McCracken's CLASS

#4

KATHLEEN, KARATE QUEEN

by Diana Oliver

BULLSEYE BOOKS
Random House 🏠 New York

For Lisa Banim, a terrific editor,
with thanks for all her creative input, her guidance,
and for originally coming up with the idea
of telling the stories of the kids
in Ms. McCracken's Class

A BULLSEYE BOOK PUBLISHED BY RANDOM HOUSE, INC.

Copyright © 1993 by Random House, Inc.
Cover design by Michaelis/Carpelis Design Associates, Inc.
Cover art copyright © 1993 by Melodye Rosales. All rights reserved
under International and Pan-American Copyright Conventions.
Published in the United States by Random House, Inc., New York,
and simultaneously in Canada
by Random House of Canada Limited, Toronto.
Library of Congress Catalog Card Number: 93-83965
ISBN: 0-679-85327-8
RL: 4.5

Manufactured in the United States of America
10 9 8 7 6 5 4 3 2 1

McCracken's Class is a trademark of Random House, Inc.

"Okay, so here's the deal." Annie leaned across the lunch table. "Yesterday, after you tricked Ronnie with your karate moves, we had this idea about starting a club. You know, to protect ourselves from Ronnie."

Kathleen nodded.

"But," Sharon put in, "*you* have to be president of the club."

"Me?" Kathleen said in disbelief. No one had ever asked her to join anything.

"We can count on you, can't we, Kathleen?" Sharon said.

"Sure, I guess so," Kathleen said.

Annie gave her a big smile. "Rosa and I have written something for the first meeting of the DO GOODERS Club."

Rosa stood up and read from a sheet of paper. "We pledge to help those who are in trouble from Ronnie Smith and other bullies. We will stick together and do our best whenever we are needed. We will meet once a week in Harry Park. All rules will be decided upon by a vote. The DO GOODERS will use their powers only for good deeds."

When Rosa finished, everyone clapped. Kathleen clapped, too. Suddenly, she was part of the group. The girls in McCracken's Class had noticed her at last!

Meet all the kids in McCracken's Class:

"Kathleen!"

Kathleen Stoppelmeyer was sitting cross-legged on her bed. As soon as she heard the door opening she pushed the money she'd been counting under her pillow.

"Hi, Mama," said Kathleen innocently.

Her mother gazed at her for a moment. "You're all dressed, I see," she said. "So why are you still up here? Come have breakfast. You'll be late for school again."

"Couldn't I stay home?" Kathleen pleaded.

Mrs. Stoppelmeyer frowned and folded her arms. "Kathleen," she said in a warning voice.

Slowly, Kathleen climbed off the bed. "Oh, Mama," she said. "Ms. McCracken is so mean. And no one in my whole class talks to me. It's like I'm invisible."

Kathleen's mother sighed. "I'm not going to go through this every morning, Kathleen.

Make your bed and come eat."

"Oh, all right," Kathleen mumbled. "I'll be there in a minute."

When her mother left the room, Kathleen shut the door. Then she picked up her pillow and looked down at all the money she'd saved. There was sixteen dollars and twenty-five cents. She knew exactly, because she counted the money whenever she added a coin to it. She was getting closer to her goal of twenty dollars—the price of a one-way train ticket back home to Cross Corners, Pennsylvania.

Home. Or at least it *was* until Papa had to sell the farm last year. What a beautiful farm it had been. Kathleen thought of the great rows of corn, the deep-mooing cows, the gentle sheep, and the always-hungry chickens.

She tilted her chin and closed her eyes. She could still hear the sounds of the farm: the animals, the swooshing leaves, the low ker-clunk of the old tractor. But the screaming police siren outside her fourth-story window was drowning them out.

Kathleen sighed. Would those horrible city sirens *ever* stop blasting? Between the ambulance, the police, and the fire sirens, they seemed to blare day and night.

She went over to her dresser and opened

the top drawer. Then she took out a slightly bent photo of her family—three older brothers, Papa, Mama, and Mama's younger sister, Aunt Jessie. They were all standing in front of the big red barn.

The farm had been in Papa's family for over a hundred years. But Papa said the farm wasn't making enough money to keep it going. He had to sell the land.

Mama's brother, Uncle Jordi, had already moved to the city and opened a trucking company. He offered Papa a job. So Kathleen's family had moved to the city last June. Now Papa drove a long truck instead of a tractor.

And Kathleen had been miserable ever since.

"Kathleen!" Mama called again.

Kathleen quickly put the pillow back over her ticket money and tossed the patchwork quilt over her bed. As she hurried toward the door, she glanced in the tall mirror. Sure enough, a strand of her long, light-blond hair had fallen loose from its elastic.

Kathleen gazed in the mirror as she fixed her braid. She had the same round, deep blue eyes as her mother. The same spray of light freckles, too. But she had her father's upturned nose. And like him, she was short and slim.

Kathleen tugged at the lace-trimmed collar of her long-sleeved white shirt. She'd loved this shirt before she moved to the city. She'd thought it was pretty, without being too frilly. She loved its red buttons and the two red birds cross-stitched on the collar. But now she knew it was all wrong. So were her jeans. They had cuffs and didn't narrow at the ankles.

None of the kids at Martin Luther King, Jr., Elementary dressed the way she did. She looked like a country bumpkin. Maybe that was why no one spoke to her much. They could tell she didn't belong.

"I'm not calling you again, Kathleen!"

"I'm coming!" Kathleen called back. She tried not to sound disrespectful.

Mama was very strict about disrespect. She always told Kathleen she came from a long line of hardworking people who obeyed their parents. Kathleen had no problem believing that. The photos in Mama's scuffed family album were all of people who looked as if they didn't smile much. Their deeply lined, weathered faces showed they'd spent lots of time working their farms.

Kathleen walked down the hall, through the living room, and into the sunny eat-in kitchen. Mama stood at the stove, making

4

pancakes and frying bacon. At the table, her three brothers, Sean, Adam, and Martin, were shoveling pancakes into their mouths. "Can I have more, Mama?" asked Adam, who was fifteen. He handed Kathleen his syrupy plate.

Kathleen frowned and handed her mother the plate. "What a hog. I haven't even had my first helping yet."

"And whose fault is that, young lady?" said Mrs. Stoppelmeyer, putting pancakes on Adam's plate. "If you didn't dawdle so much you'd be finished by now, too." She handed the plate back to Adam. "The usual, Kathleen?" she asked.

"Yes, thank you," said Kathleen, nodding. "Two, please."

"'Morning, everyone." Mr. Stoppelmeyer gave his usual greeting as he came into the kitchen.

"'Morning, Pop," said Sean, who was thirteen.

Mr. Stoppelmeyer frowned at him. Sean knew his father didn't like being called Pop, but Sean said "Papa" sounded goofy. "Good morning, son," Mr. Stoppelmeyer replied.

Kathleen sat with her brothers and her father. Mrs. Stoppelmeyer ate standing up at the counter. The big wooden table they'd brought with them didn't fit in the kitchen so they'd bought a smaller one. Now there wasn't room for all of them to sit together.

When they were done, Kathleen went out the door with her brothers. They walked down two flights of dark stairs. At the second-floor landing, Kathleen knocked hard on the door marked 3-L, just as she did every morning.

Kathleen waited as her brothers went down ahead of her. In a few moments, she heard the clanking sound of several locks being unlocked. Then a pretty woman with long blond hair and big, sleepy blue eyes stood in the doorway wrapped in a terry-cloth robe. "'Morning, Aunt Jessie!" Kathleen sang out.

"'Mornin', sweetie," Aunt Jessie replied through a yawn. Aunt Jessie was Mama's youngest sister. She was only twenty-five. Just before the family moved to the city, Aunt Jessie and Tom Smithers, the man she was going to marry, had broken up. Heartbroken, Aunt Jessie had moved to the city with them. Luckily, she was able to find a small apartment in the same building.

"Thanks for the wake-up call," said Aunt Jessie.

"No problem," Kathleen replied as she

hurried down the stairs after her brothers. "Have a good day at work."

Aunt Jessie laughed. "Fat chance," she said as she shut the door. Kathleen knew Aunt Jessie hated her job at Beekman's Department Store. But Kathleen always wished her a good day anyway.

Outside, Kathleen ran to catch up with her brothers as they headed down Willow Street. *What a pretty name for such an ugly street,* Kathleen thought. Brick apartment buildings and row houses stood side by side. The front yards were cemented in. Some of them were neatly kept. Others were full of old junk.

It had rained the night before. Big puddles sat in the cracks of the broken sidewalk. Today was garbage pickup day, so the curbs were lined with dented metal trash cans and plastic trash bags. The cold late-fall wind had blown the lids off the cans and scattered garbage across the street and sidewalk. "Gross!" said Kathleen as an empty, wet, muddy potato chip bag caught on her leg.

"Oh, stop complaining," said Adam. "That's all you've done since we got to Parkside."

"I have not," Kathleen replied. "You guys have it easy. You're big football stars at school. Everyone pays attention to you."

"Hey, when you're the best, you're the best," laughed Sean. He tugged down the rim of his blue baseball cap.

"Is that what you tell Megan Malone?" Martin teased. "I heard you talking to her on the phone again last night."

Sean turned pink. "Hey, *she* called me. What was I supposed to do? Hang up on her?"

"Seanie's in love! Seanie's in love," Adam sang out.

"Shut up!" Sean snarled. "All *you* think about is Teresa Tuzmarti. She's a senior and she has a boyfriend."

"Yeah," put in Martin, who was also a senior. "You don't want to mess with Vinnie."

"Ah-ha, Adam's a loser at love," Sean taunted.

"You're a loser at everything," Adam shot back, grabbing Sean's cap from his head. Sean chased Adam up the street, leaving Kathleen alone with Martin.

Martin was Kathleen's oldest brother. He wasn't very tall, but he was a terrific athlete. He could tear his way across a football field like the wind. He was also handsome, with thick blond hair and deep blue eyes. Martin never teased Kathleen or said disgusting things. Not like her other brothers. "Teresa

8

Tuzmarti's sister is in my class," she told him.

"Oh, yeah? Is she a pal of yours?" Martin asked.

Kathleen shook her head. "Annie's nice, but she's not my friend."

"Why not?" Martin asked.

"I don't know," Kathleen shrugged. "I haven't really made any friends yet." They walked along a few minutes without speaking. "You hate it here, too, don't you, Martin?" she asked after a while.

"Not so much anymore," he answered. "Parkside has a much better football team than we had at Cross Corners. And the kids here are okay, once you get used to them."

"Not in my class," Kathleen said. "And *you* don't have Ms. McCracken for a teacher."

"I hear she's pretty tough," Martin admitted.

Kathleen was impressed. "They talk about Ms. McCracken all the way over in the high school?"

Martin smiled. "Yeah. It's like some kids never got over having her for a teacher back in the fifth grade. They act like it was the worst year of their lives. She's real strict, huh?"

Kathleen nodded. "She's scary-looking,

too. Her hair is orange and all high up so it looks like a bunch of bees are going to come out of it any second."

They caught up to Sean and Adam on the corner of busy Grant Avenue. The boys had to go in the opposite direction from Kathleen to get to the junior high and high school. "Don't be late for class, all right?" Martin told her. "If the school calls Mama again, she's going to have a breakdown or something."

Kathleen hooted. "Mama? No way!"

"Just be on time," Martin said. "Mama doesn't need any more headaches right now. And neither does Papa."

"Oh, all right," Kathleen agreed.

Her brothers went on their way and Kathleen started down Grant toward Martin Luther King, Jr., Elementary. Half a block ahead, she saw some kids from her class. Annie Tuzmarti was walking with John Jerome and Rosa Santiago. Behind them were Lori Silver, Sharon Fuller, and Sasha Sommers. And Sylvie Levine, Carlos Ortega, and Kareem Jackson were almost at the end of the block. Kathleen watched as each group reached Newton's Newsstand and ducked inside.

Kathleen stopped walking. By the time they bought their stuff, she'd probably be right at Newton's. Then they'd all come out, joking and whispering, and there she'd be.

Would they speak to her? Sometimes Sylvie smiled and said hi, but that was about it. They weren't mean to her exactly. But it was as if she didn't exist. They'd all probably known each other since kindergarten. Why should they want to make friends with a new kid?

But she couldn't just pass by her class-mates without saying anything. That would seem snobby.

No, the best bet was to cut through the park and avoid them altogether. William Henry Harrison Park—or Harry Park, as everyone in Parkside called it—was the reason Kathleen was always late for school.

Kathleen looked both ways and ran across the street. Then she hurried along the side-walk outside a low stone wall until she reached the main entrance.

Kathleen's spirits rose as she entered the park. To Kathleen, the park was the only beautiful place in the city. It was hilly, with shady patches of thick, full trees.

She walked past the kiddie park, with its small swings and colorful jungle gym. Baby-sitters, moms, and a few dads were already starting to stroll the little kids in. She went on, up a hill, until she came to a large, open field. If she squinted with her eyes almost shut, she could pretend she was home.

Kathleen stopped to smell the wet air. Above, a large bird screeched as it circled the north end of the park. For a moment, Kathleen didn't hear a single siren.

Feeling light and happy, Kathleen ran into the field, the wet grass squishing under her sneakers. She headed straight for the trees.

Grabbing a low-hanging branch, she kicked up her legs and pulled herself up into a large oak. With surefooted ease, she climbed the tree. Then she leaned against the cool, strong trunk and gazed out over the park.

She sat there for a while, feeling like a part of nature.

Suddenly, in the distance, she heard a siren beginning to blare. *Oh, no!* Kathleen thought, scrambling down the tree. How long had she been sitting there? She was going to be late for school again!

Kathleen hurried out of the park. She could see Martin Luther King, Jr., Elementary on the other side of the street. The school was a large, ugly square building with wide, green doors.

Kathleen breathed a sigh of relief as she crossed the street. Kids were still outside in the schoolyard. She'd made it on time after all!

But almost as soon as she came through the entrance in the chain-link fence, Kathleen stopped dead. Ronnie Smith was only a few feet away, picking on a small boy.

Ronnie was the school bully. And she was a girl. But she was just as mean as Ethan Hawks, the bully at Kathleen's old school.

Ronnie was taller than most of the other kids. She had short, choppy brown hair and sly, coppery eyes. The white scar on her top lip made her look even meaner. Ronnie was in McCracken's class, but even the sixth graders—the oldest kids at school—were afraid of her.

Ronnie hung around with two other girls, Cheryl and Jodi. They weren't particularly nice, either. Jodi had drab blond hair that looked as if she hardly ever washed it. She was skinny and nervous, always moving, jiggling, or checking over her shoulder. Cheryl had stringy black hair. A wad of gum was always in her mouth. Her dull blue eyes were heavy-lidded, and she usually wore an expression of total boredom.

"Okay, punk," Ronnie growled, sneering at the third-grade boy. He stood under the basketball hoops surrounded by his friends. He was small for his age, but he wore a brave expression. "Me and my friends are gonna use the hoops now," Ronnie told him. "So beat it."

"We were playing a game," the small boy objected. His friends nodded.

Ronnie lifted the boy up by his shirt. "If you want to live, you'll get outta my way," she said. Then she tossed him onto the ground.

The other third-graders helped him up, looking frightened. *Why doesn't someone stand up to that girl?* Kathleen wondered.

Just then, Kathleen saw John Jerome approach Ronnie. John had brown, spiky hair and big brown eyes. He was one of the cool fifth grade kids. He was tall, but not as big as Ronnie.

Several feet away, his friends stood in a group watching. Annie Tuzmarti had her arms folded. Sharon Fuller had turned away as if she couldn't bear to look. Kareem Jackson stood with his legs apart, as if he was ready to jump in and help John. Although he was named for basketball star Kareem Abdul-Jabbar, Kareem was the shortest boy in McCracken's class. He probably wouldn't be much help if John really needed him.

"Why don't you pick on somebody your own size?" John challenged Ronnie.

"Get lost, Jerome," Ronnie snarled.

"*You* get lost, *Veronica!*" he shot back.

A hush fell over the schoolyard. Calling Ronnie Smith by her real name was the most dangerous thing anyone could do. It was like yanking a tiger's tail on purpose.

Ronnie lunged forward and shoved John. He went flying backward, waving his arms like a windmill.

Kathleen stepped closer to the fight. She wanted to see what would happen.

John caught his balance. Then he raced

toward Ronnie like a football player.

Bam!

He hit Ronnie full force.

Suddenly Ronnie was flying in Kathleen's direction. Before Kathleen could jump out of the way, Ronnie smashed into her with a sickening thud. The two of them tumbled onto the hard ground.

"Hey, moron," Ronnie snarled at Kathleen. "Get out of my face."

Kathleen gasped, trying hard to catch her breath. The wind had been knocked right out of her. "I wasn't in your face," she panted, slowly getting to her feet.

Ronnie scrambled up quickly. "What did you say?" she asked.

"I said, I wasn't in your face," Kathleen replied angrily.

Ronnie grabbed Kathleen's shoulder. "I don't like your tone of voice," she said. "Say you're sorry, or you're dead meat."

There was no way Kathleen was going to apologize to Ronnie Smith. She'd never let Ethan Hawks push her around. And she wasn't going to let Ronnie do it, either. Kathleen stood silently, glowering right back at Ronnie.

Ronnie shook her roughly. "Apologize or die!"

Kathleen heard John shout. "Leave her alone!" John was right behind Ronnie. But Kathleen was only dimly aware of him as she stared into Ronnie's narrowed eyes. Kathleen's heart was pounding. But she was stubborn. Aunt Jessie always told her so. And she was angry, too.

Ronnie made the first move. She reached out and yanked Kathleen's hair, pulling her head back.

Kathleen reacted with pure instinct—*and* three and a half years of karate lessons.

She grabbed Ronnie's arm with two hands. Then she stuck out her leg and neatly threw Ronnie over it. Ronnie fell right onto her back and into a puddle.

"You...you!" Ronnie sputtered.

The kids in the schoolyard cheered.

Kathleen paid no attention to them. She backed up quickly and spread her feet wide. Then she held her two hands in front of her in a karate stance.

Ronnie got back up and came toward Kathleen. Her clothes were wet, but she didn't seem to care. She hunched over and balled her hands into huge, tight fists.

"*Eeee-iii-aaa-ayh!*" Kathleen leapt in the air and kicked out her left foot in Ronnie's direction. She didn't really want to hit

Ronnie. She just wanted to scare her.

"Look at that!" someone cried.

"Awesome!" another kid said.

The next thing Kathleen heard was the sound of hands clapping sharply. "What on earth is going on here?" a familiar angry voice demanded.

Kathleen turned and found herself staring at Ms. McCracken. The spray on the tall, thin teacher's bright orange hair made it look like a helmet. Her brown tweed overcoat flapped in the wet breeze.

Speechless, Kathleen looked back at Ronnie, then at John. They, too, were frozen where they stood.

The first bell rang and broke the chilling moment. "All right, you three," said Ms. McCracken. "Come with me."

Ronnie glared at Kathleen as she began to trail after Ms. McCracken. Kathleen looked down at the ground.

Mr. Ramone, the short, broad assistant principal, blew his silver whistle. All the classes started heading toward the big, green doors of the school. "You three, stay with me," said Ms. McCracken.

Kathleen felt as though the entire school was staring at her. Was this better than feeling invisible? Or worse?

She squared her shoulders and tried to walk tall. A piece of hair had come loose from one of her braids and fallen across her face. She also realized that the elbow of her red jacket had torn.

Ms. McCracken walked with them as far as their classroom on the second floor, Room 206. The class filed in, but Ms. McCracken signaled Ronnie, John, and Kathleen to Room 208 next door.

They went into the empty classroom and took seats. "Take out a sheet of loose-leaf paper," Ms. McCracken told them. "I want you to write a five-page essay on why physical violence never solves anything. You have until noon to finish. You may use examples from history and from your own life."

Ms. McCracken stood with her arms folded as they got out their notebooks. "These essays will be taken home and signed by your parents. At the top of the page, I want you to write: *This is a punishment assignment.* I want the essays on my desk tomorrow morning. I also expect you to make up the lessons you miss today by consulting with another classmate. Is all of this clear?"

"Yes, Ms. McCracken," Kathleen and John said together. Ronnie was silent.

"If I see any more fighting I will take

19

stronger action. Now begin."

The teacher walked up and down the aisles a few times. Kathleen didn't know what to write, so she began writing her name very slowly.

Finally Ms. McCracken left the room. "I'll be back to check on you three in a few minutes," she called over her shoulder.

Kathleen slumped in her seat. Her parents were going to be really angry. They'd told her when she started taking karate that they didn't want her getting into fights. She'd sworn she wouldn't, and she never had—until today.

They'd be mad at Aunt Jessie, too. Aunt Jessie had a brown belt in karate. That was one step away from being a black belt, the highest degree in karate. Mama hadn't liked the idea of Kathleen taking karate lessons at all. Aunt Jessie had talked her into it.

When Kathleen was seven, her Aunt Jessie had taken her to the martial arts school. It was called a dojo, but it was just a converted barn. Kathleen had been so thrilled!

She and her brothers had always watched martial arts movies on Saturday morning TV. She loved the way the actors moved, and how strong and brave they were.

Now she looked down at the blank piece of paper in front of her. What could she write? She knew violence didn't solve problems. Her teacher, Mr. Funakoshi, had always told them that the martial arts were to be used only for self-defense. Well, hadn't she done that? She didn't think she should have to apologize. Neither should John, for that matter. All he'd done was try to stick up for someone.

Kathleen thought of Ronnie. She wanted to write: *Sometimes violence gets the real violent people to leave you alone*. But she had a pretty strong idea that wasn't what Ms. McCracken was looking for. Kathleen sighed and rested her chin on her hands.

The scratching sound of chalk on the blackboard made her look up. Ronnie's seat was near the side blackboard. She was writing something on the board. Then she leaned back so that Kathleen could see what it said.

The writing was very small. Ronnie grinned as Kathleen squinted to read it. Slowly the letters came into focus. Ronnie had written: "U R Ded Meet!!!!!!"

Kathleen knit her brows. What did that mean? Suddenly she realized. Dead meat. *You are dead meat!*

3

Kathleen stood in front of Ms. McCracken and tried not to tremble. It was lunchtime and she still hadn't started her essay.

The teacher had sent John and Ronnie off to the lunchroom, but she'd kept Kathleen behind. "Why didn't you write this essay, Ms. Stoppelmeyer?" Ms. McCracken demanded.

"I needed more time," Kathleen said.

Ms. McCracken's eyes narrowed. "You haven't written one word."

It was time for the truth. "I don't think I did anything wrong," Kathleen blurted out.

Two red splotches formed on Ms. McCracken's pale cheeks. Kathleen had seen those splotches before. They were a sure sign that Ms. McCracken was getting angry.

"You don't think fighting in the schoolyard is wrong?" she asked.

Kathleen held firm. "It was self-defense."

"Did Ms. Smith strike you?" Ms. McCracken asked.

"She pulled my hair," Kathleen said. "And she was picking on some other kids, too. Smaller kids."

"You're quite a bit smaller than Ms. Smith yourself," Ms. McCracken said.

"Yes, but I'm a good fighter. I have a green belt in karate," said Kathleen.

"I see." Ms. McCracken raised one of her thin eyebrows. "Was it necessary to *drop kick* Ms. Smith?"

Kathleen looked away. "Yes."

"All right, then," Ms. McCracken said. "I want an essay from you on the art of negotiation."

"What's that?" Kathleen asked.

"It means solving problems through talk rather than physical action," Ms. McCracken said. "It's something I recommend you think about."

"Do I have to write that part about the punishment assignment?" Kathleen asked.

"No."

Kathleen sighed with relief.

"You won't have to *write* the words 'punishment assignment' yourself," Ms. McCracken continued, "because I've just received the special stamp I ordered in the mail. It was in my school mailbox this morning." Ms. McCracken took a rubber stamp and a stamp pad from the desk drawer. "Open your loose-leaf binder, please."

Kathleen opened her binder. Ms. McCracken inked her stamp and then stamped it at the top of the page. In red-ink capital letters, the stamp printed:

PUNISHMENT ESSAY
PARENT: PLEASE SIGN HERE_____

Only McCracken would have a stamp like that, thought Kathleen miserably. There was no way she could tell her parents this was a special homework assignment that had to be signed.

"Now go to lunch," said Ms. McCracken.

Kathleen left the classroom but was too upset to go to the cafeteria. Instead she ducked into the girls' room on the second floor. She stayed there, sitting on a toilet with the lid shut, until she heard the bell ring for the end of lunch.

All afternoon, Kathleen wondered what her classmates thought of her now. So far, no one had said one word to her. Did they think she was some kind of violent nut? Being invisible had been better than this.

Every afternoon, Ms. McCracken's class

switched classrooms with Ms. Rivers's class. Ms. Rivers taught English and reading, and Ms. McCracken taught science, math, and social studies.

Usually, Kathleen liked Ms. Rivers's lessons. Ms. Rivers always made them seem interesting. And she was a lot nicer than Ms. McCracken, too. But now Kathleen stared down at her open literature book. She thought hard about how she might have talked her way out of her fight with Ronnie. No great ideas came to her. Finally she gave up.

After school, Kathleen took the long way home. She didn't want to run into Ronnie Smith. Even though she knew she could beat Ronnie in a fair fight, she wasn't sure Ronnie would play fair.

She cut through the south end of Harry Park and came out on Harrison South. From there, she made her way through the Parkside Cemetery.

The wet wind was blowing again. Kathleen turned up the collar of her jacket as she walked along the cement path that wound through the graves. The sky was clouding over again. She didn't want to get caught in a storm, but she didn't want to go home, either.

With her hands jammed in her pockets, Kathleen began to wander about looking at the gravestones. Some dated back to the late 1600's.

She stopped at the grand monument—an arch with three chubby stone cherubs at the top—that marked the grave of Zoe Montgomery. She was a famous movie star from the 1920's. There were always lots of flowers on her grave. Desdemona DuMonde, one of the girls in McCracken's class, was always talking about Zoe Montgomery. She even drew a picture of her once during art class. Desdemona was always telling everyone she wanted to be an actress someday. Kathleen wondered if she'd placed any of these flowers on her grave.

Suddenly a twig cracked behind Kathleen. She froze. Had Ronnie followed her here?

She turned around sharply.

"Well, what do you know," said Aunt Jessie, smiling. "I can't believe I've run into you in a cemetery."

"What are you doing here?" Kathleen asked. She was surprised but very happy to see her aunt.

"Didn't you know that I'm the world's biggest Zoe Montgomery fan?" Aunt Jessie said.

"No," Kathleen admitted.

Aunt Jessie smiled. "Well, I am. No joke. I love her old movies. She was a really gutsy, funny, independent lady. She wrote her own scripts and directed some of her own movies, too."

"She sounds really cool," said Kathleen.

"She was," said Aunt Jessie. "The first time I came to see her grave here in Parkside I got the feeling that she was around and could see me."

"You did?" Kathleen shivered.

"I know it sounds crazy," said Aunt Jessie. "But it was like visiting an old friend."

"It doesn't sound crazy," said Kathleen. "It sounds nice." She hesitated. "Aunt Jessie," she said, "do you ever miss Cross Corners?"

"You know, Kathleen, I do. I never expected to, either. Sometimes I really want to go back there."

"I want to go back, too," Kathleen told her. "I've saved most of the money for a train ticket home. More than half. And when I get enough, I'm going."

Aunt Jessie looked sad, but she smiled at Kathleen. "Hey, sweetie," she said. "Home is where your family is."

Kathleen shook her head. "Home is Cross Corners. It will never be here in the city.

Never in a zillion years."

"I know how you feel," said Aunt Jessie with a sigh.

Just then, Kathleen had a wonderful idea. "How about if you adopt me?"

"*What?*" Aunt Jessie sounded shocked.

"Okay, never mind," said Kathleen. "But what if we went back to Cross Corners together? You could take care of me!"

"I don't think your parents would go for that," Aunt Jessie pointed out.

"They might," Kathleen insisted. Lately her parents hardly seemed to notice her at all. Papa worked all the time. And Mama always seemed to have something else on her mind. Besides, maybe if Papa made some money from truck driving, he'd be able to buy back the farm. Until then, she'd be able to keep an eye on it for him in Cross Corners.

"You could talk Mama into letting me go back with you," Kathleen said. "Just like you talked her into letting me take karate."

Aunt Jessie's face grew thoughtful. "I don't know, Kath. I wouldn't mind having you live with me. I'd love that. I just don't know, though. It would take some time, for one thing."

"Why?"

"Well, for starters, because I'm broke."

"But you're working," Kathleen pressed.

Aunt Jessie shook her head. "Not as of this afternoon, I'm not. They fired me for telling some rude customer to go take a hike."

"You said that?" Kathleen gasped.

Aunt Jessie nodded. "Yep." Then she laughed sadly. "I hated that stupid job. But I don't know what to do now. I can't very well ask your parents for a loan. They have their own problems. I guess that's why I came out here to see Zoe. I felt like I needed someone to talk to."

Kathleen put her arm around Aunt Jessie. "You have me."

"I know," Aunt Jessie said.

They stood for a moment looking at the fat angels on Zoe Montgomery's grave. Kathleen felt terrible. Aunt Jessie was always full of life and fun. It was awful to see her so down.

"All right," Kathleen said finally. "We'll just have to wait until you get another job before we can go. I know it won't take long. Living together will be lots of fun. "

"Hold on," said Aunt Jessie. "I didn't say I was going to do this."

"But we are, aren't we?" Kathleen said.

"*Maybe.* I'll have to think about it."

"All right!" Kathleen cheered. Whenever Aunt Jessie said she'd think about something, she almost always did it.

Aunt Jessie laughed. "Hey, I didn't say yes."

"I know," Kathleen agreed happily. "You have to think about it. That's okay."

"Fine," said Aunt Jessie. "Now how about us cutting back through the park? We can make a stop at Ice Cream Heaven."

"But you're broke," Kathleen reminded her. "And so am I."

"Oh, I've got a few cents left," said Aunt Jessie. "Enough for two Rocky Road cones, anyway." She began to walk back across the wet grass toward Harry Park. "Let the landlord wait for his rent," she cried out. "We must have ice cream today!"

"Ice cream today!" Kathleen echoed. But it wasn't the thought of a Rocky Road cone that made her feel so happy. She was going home!

4

The next day, Kathleen handed in her essay to Ms. McCracken. The teacher eyed it with a frown. Kathleen gulped hard. Sean had signed their father's name on the parent's signature line. She'd thought he'd done a pretty good job.

"I've seen your father's signature before," Ms. McCracken said. "He's signed several permission slips. I always pay attention to a parent's signature. And this one looks different. Why is that?"

Frosty fear began to creep up Kathleen's back. How could she have been so stupid to think she'd ever fool eagle-eyed McCracken?

"Um..." Kathleen stammered. She didn't usually lie. She wasn't very good at it, and she hated doing it. "I think he had too many beers last night," she said, remembering the answer Sean had suggested. It was a total lie.

Their father never drank beer or any alcohol at all.

But the lie seemed to work. "All right," said Ms. McCracken quickly. She stuffed the essay in her desk drawer. "Take your seat, please."

Kathleen sat down in her seat behind Sharon Fuller. To her surprise, Sharon passed her a note. It was the very first note Kathleen had received from any of her classmates. She held it under her desk and opened it up.

Kathleen peered at Sharon's fat, loopy script. *Can you meet me at lunch? I have something very important to talk to you about.*

Meet Sharon for lunch? Kathleen never sat with anyone at lunch. Usually she took a book and read it while she ate.

She wasn't even sure she liked Sharon Fuller all that much. Her dark hair was always perfect, and she wore trendy outfits with bows, sparkles, and sequins. But Sharon was fairly popular. There had to be *something* nice about her.

Sure, Kathleen scribbled back on the bottom of Sharon's note. She refolded it and dropped it over Sharon's shoulder when McCracken was writing on the blackboard.

From then on, Kathleen began to feel nervous. What would she and Sharon talk about?

When the lunch bell finally rang, Kathleen walked with Sharon to the lunchroom. "So what's so important?" she asked.

"You'll see," Sharon said, hooking her arm through Kathleen's. She led her to a table near the back of the cafeteria. Some girls from their class were already sitting there: Annie Tuzmarti, Rosa Santiago, Sylvie Levine, Desdemona DuMonde, Sasha Sommers, and Lori Silver. "Meet the DO GOODERS!" Sharon announced grandly.

"The what?" Kathleen asked.

"DO just stands for do," Sharon explained. "But GOODERS stands for Girls' Order of Defenders, Especially Ronnie Smith."

"Oh," said Kathleen. She still didn't get it.

"If you think of anything the DO could stand for, let us know," Sylvie added.

"All right," said Kathleen.

"Have a seat," said Sharon. She pulled out a metal chair for Kathleen as if the cafeteria were her home. Kathleen sat down and smiled shyly at the girls. They all smiled back.

"Okay, here's the deal," said Annie. "We started thinking about something yesterday.

33

There's no reason we should all be so afraid of Ronnie. I mean, *I'm* not that afraid of her, but—"

"You are so," Sharon interrupted.

"Well, not as much as I used to be," Annie said. "Anyway, a lot of kids *are* really afraid of her. It's terrible."

"She tried to beat me up once," Rosa put in. "If Annie hadn't been there to help me, I don't know what would have happened."

"What did you do?" Kathleen asked Annie.

Annie shrugged. "I just acted tough," said Annie. "I said I'd take her on, but she probably would have creamed me if we'd really had a fight. She's huge."

Annie nodded toward Ronnie, who was lumbering toward a table with Jodi and Cheryl. Kathleen understood what Annie meant. Ronnie *was* very large.

"And she's mean," added Lori Silver.

"Carlos and I had trouble with her, too," said Sylvie.

"But you handled her great, Kathleen," Desdemona said. "It was awesome. You're like Bruce Lee and the Karate Kid and the Teenage Mutant Ninja Turtles all rolled up into one." Her dark eyes flashed and she threw her arms out dramatically as she spoke.

"Okay, so here's what we're going to do," Annie leaned forward. "Yesterday, after you taught Ronnie a lesson, I had this idea about starting a club. You know, to protect ourselves from Ronnie. I talked to Sharon and Rosa about it, and they talked to everyone else. We decided to ask you to meet us here today to talk things over. We want to start the DO GOODERS club to defend everyone against Ronnie and her gang."

"Good idea," Kathleen agreed.

"But," said Sharon, "we can only do it if you agree to be the president of the club."

"Me?" Kathleen cried in disbelief. No one had ever asked her to join anything.

"We'd help, of course," said Annie quickly. "I mean, we'd all be there, but you'd be the leader. We could have regular meetings and everything."

"I guess that would be okay," said Kathleen slowly. Should she tell them she wasn't planning to be in Parkside that much longer? She decided against it.

"All right!" Desdemona cheered.

"We knew we could count on you," said Sharon.

Annie gave Kathleen a big smile. "Rosa and I have written something for the opening of the DO GOODERS club."

Rosa stood up. She was very short with long, dark hair. Even though she didn't look as nerdy as she had back in September, thanks to Annie, Rosa still dressed in plaid pants and white shirts. *I wear white shirts, too*, Kathleen reminded herself. Did the other kids think she was a geek like Rosa?

"The first meeting of the DO GOODERS club is about to start," Rosa read from a sheet of paper. "We pledge to help those who are in trouble from Ronnie Smith and other bullies. We will stick together and do our best whenever we are needed. We will meet once a week in Harry Park. All rules will be decided by a vote. All new members will be agreed upon by a vote, too. The DO GOODERS will use their powers only for good deeds."

When she was done, all the girls clapped. Kathleen clapped too.

"Okay, let's eat," said Annie. Everyone at the table headed quickly for the lunch line.

Kathleen was surprised and delighted when the other DO GOODERS started asking her all kinds of questions.

"What's it like living on a farm?" Lori asked.

"What kind of martial art do you take, karate, judo, or what?" asked Annie.

Kathleen told them about her life on the

farm. She also told about Mr. Funakoshi and her karate lessons. They all seemed very interested.

"Do you have one of those whitish karate outfits?" Sharon wanted to know. "Do they make them in different colors? If they make them in pink, I want one. I look horrible in that off-whitish color."

"We should all get those outfits," Desdemona said.

Sylvie laughed. "You just want to wear a costume," she told her.

"As long as they're not that whitish color," said Sharon.

"So where do you get those outfits?" Desdemona asked. "I definitely want one." She began chopping the air with her hands, fighting an imaginary enemy. "Ha! Ha! Take that, you creep!"

It went on like that all through lunch. Kathleen had a hard time keeping up with all the girls' questions.

"Do you have a belt color?" Annie asked.

"I'm a green belt," Kathleen told her. "It's one of the lower levels. My aunt is a brown belt. That's the belt below a black belt, which is the best."

"I read something about belts once," Rosa put in. "A long time ago, karate students started out with white belts that matched their robes. But the longer they studied, the darker the belts got. A black belt is really just a worn, dirty belt that got that way from lots of hard use."

Kathleen nodded. Mr. Funakoshi had told them the same thing.

"Yuck!" said Sharon. "Who'd want to wear a dirty belt?" She turned to Kathleen. "Were you the only girl in your class?"

"No. There was one other girl, my friend Lizzy," Kathleen told her.

"But mostly guys, right?" Sharon pressed.

"Yes," Kathleen replied. "Mostly guys."

"I'm going to ask my mom if I can study karate," said Sharon.

"You're so boy-crazy," said Lori.

"So?" Sharon said shrugging.

Kathleen was done with her tuna melt before everyone else. She wasn't quite sure what to do. Should she stay there and wait for the others? Or should she leave? She was having a great time. But she didn't usually sit with any of these girls. Would they want her to go out to the schoolyard with them?

She decided to get up and go.

"Where are you going?" Desdemona asked.

"Um...I don't know," Kathleen admitted.

"You usually read at lunchtime, don't you?" Rosa asked.

"What are you reading?" asked Annie. She sounded interested.

"Well, I was reading *The Secret Garden*," Kathleen said, "but I finished it last night. I'm not exactly reading anything right now." She hesitated. "I only read in the lunchroom when there's no one to, um...Well, you know. When there's nothing much else to do."

"See, I told you she didn't like reading by herself all the time," Sharon said to the others.

Kathleen felt a blush warm her face.

"Sharon, don't be a twit," Desdemona scolded. She turned to Kathleen. "All Sharon means is that you seem to like being by yourself. We weren't sure if you'd want to do this club thing."

"I don't mean to keep to myself," Kathleen mumbled.

"You crossed the street to avoid us the other day on Grant Avenue," Sharon said.

"Sharon!" Annie wailed.

"Well, she did," Sharon insisted.

"I know," Kathleen admitted. "But I wasn't being snobby. I just wasn't sure if...if..."

"It doesn't matter," Desdemona broke in.

"We're all friends now. And you're even president of the DO GOODERS club. What could be better than that?"

Nothing, Kathleen decided. *Absolutely nothing.*

"You've never had Luigi's pizza?" Annie gasped.

Kathleen shook her head. School had just gotten out. The other DO GOODERS had invited Kathleen to walk home with them. It was the first time Kathleen had ever walked home with any kids from her class. "My mother usually cooks," Kathleen explained.

"Your mother *cooks*?" Desdemona sounded shocked. "Where does she find the time?"

Kathleen shrugged. "I don't know." Her mother had never worked outside the house. But ever since they moved to the city, she'd been looking for a job. All she'd been able to find so far was a job selling magazines over the phone. She didn't sell too many of them, but she tried really hard.

"Well, you're in for treat," said Sylvie as they neared the pizza parlor. "Luigi's makes the best pizza anywhere."

"My family doesn't eat much pizza either," Rosa told Kathleen. "My parents say it's junk food and a waste of money."

"That reminds me," Annie said, frowning. "I don't have much money on me."

"Me, neither," said Kathleen. She was glad she wasn't the only one without money. Every spare cent she had was under her pillow for the train ticket fund.

"No problem," said Sharon. "I have ten dollars left from my birthday money."

"That's enough for a large pie," said Lori. "We could all pay you back later."

Sharon waved a hand. "Don't worry about it. Let's go."

The girls went into the wide, bright pizzeria. It was filled with red booths against dark green walls. They ordered a large pie—half pepperoni and half plain—at the counter. Then they squeezed into a booth. Kathleen sat wedged between Rosa and Sasha. She was really starting to feel like part of the group.

"I can't wait for this pizza," said Annie. "My sister, Teresa, never lets me get pepperoni. She says it gives her zits."

"My brother Adam likes your sister," Kathleen confided.

"Teresa?" Annie snorted. "All the boys like

her. But she's in love with Vinnie."

Kathleen nodded. "My other brother told him that."

"How many brothers do you have?" asked Sasha. She looked surprised.

"Three," said Kathleen.

"We had no idea you were so interesting," said Sharon. "We thought you were just this quiet little mouse with nothing much to say."

"Sharon!" Annie scolded once again.

"It's all right to be quiet," said Rosa. Kathleen knew Rosa was fairly shy herself. If she wasn't friends with Annie, she probably wouldn't have been in the DO GOODERS. And Sasha Sommers was pretty quiet, too.

"I'm not always quiet," Kathleen said. "I don't think I am, anyway."

"Of course you're not," said Desdemona. "I just thought you were snobby. Or maybe you just liked being by yourself."

How could anyone have thought that? Kathleen wondered. Who really liked to be alone? She'd kept to herself because she didn't think anyone wanted to bother with her. And no one had ever been very friendly.

"Well, how many people do we know who are human weapons?" Sharon said. She smiled at Kathleen.

"I'm not a human weapon," said Kathleen.

"Oh, you know what I mean," Sharon said with a wave of her hand.

Just then, a man in a long white apron delivered the pizza to their table. Annie immediately reached for a slice.

Kathleen had had pizza before, but this one looked different. The pizza in Cross Corners was thicker and less greasy. She wasn't sure if she'd like this pie.

Everyone was starting to pull hot, gooey slices from the pie when the bell over Luigi's doorway rang. Kathleen glanced up and her heart flip-flopped. Ronnie, Cheryl, and Jodi had just walked in.

"Here comes trouble," muttered Desdemona.

"Ignore them," Sylvie advised.

Ronnie walked right up to their table and looked down at the pie. "Three slices left," she said. "I guess you guys wouldn't mind if we took them, huh?"

"Guess again," said Annie.

Ronnie glared at her. "I should have pounded some sense into you that day at the library, Tuzmarti."

"Too bad you ran away like a coward," Annie shot back. "*Veronica.*"

Ronnie's eyes narrowed dangerously. "I don't know why I let you live, Tuzmarti."

"Because you were scared," Annie replied.

"Scared of you? No way! You're just playing tough because you're friends with the karate geek here." Ronnie nodded toward Kathleen.

All the girls turned to stare at Kathleen. She wished they hadn't done that. They probably expected her to do something. After all, she was the president of the DO GOODERS. "Who are you calling a geek?" she challenged Ronnie.

"I'm calling *you* a geek, geek," said Ronnie.

Everyone continued to stare at Kathleen. She couldn't just sit there. Slowly she got up.

"Do you want to say that again outside?" she asked. She'd once heard Martin say that to a guy who tried to pick a fight at the Cross Corners Diner. The guy had just glared at Martin and walked away.

"No problem, dead meat geek," said Ronnie.

"Let's go," said Annie, pushing her chair back. Kathleen knew there was nothing else she could do. She remembered the essay she'd written for Ms. McCracken. But this was no time to be negotiating.

"But what about our pizza?" Sharon asked.

"I'll get it packed up to go," Lori said.

There was no turning back now. To chicken out would mean disappointing her new friends. After all, she *was* the president of the DO GOODERS club.

With her head high and her heart pounding, Kathleen walked out of Luigi's. Mr. Funakoshi always said that a person's mind was his greatest weapon. He told his students they had to get a mental picture of themselves as great warriors. They had to imagine themselves winning the fight.

As they walked toward the park, Kathleen tried to do all those things. Then she thought about Ti Lung in her favorite martial arts movie, *Five Masters of Death*. His face looked serious, but not worried. He showed no fear. And once he started to fight you knew why. He seemed to float along the ground on a cushion of air, ready to twirl and leap at any moment. Ti Lung did *kung fu* rather than karate, but the idea was the same. He was sure and quick, a master fighter.

Still thinking about Ti Lung, Kathleen walked past the kiddie park and stepped out into the clearing. Her new friends trailed behind her. Ronnie, Cheryl, and Jodi were waiting for them.

"You're going to get it now," Desdemona told Ronnie.

46

Ronnie just glared at her.

"Yeah. You don't scare us anymore, Smith!" said Sharon boldly. "We've got protection now."

Several feet into the clearing, Kathleen stopped. She took a fighting stance with her feet wide to keep herself balanced. She held one hand slightly curved in front of her face and the other in a fist at her waist.

"Oh, don't make me laugh," Ronnie sneered.

Kathleen didn't move. She didn't even blink. Mr. Funakoshi had trained her not to be thrown off by anything an opponent said.

"Get her, Kathleen!" Annie shouted.

"Might as well get this over with quick," Ronnie said coolly. She peeled off her faded denim jacket. Then she came up to Kathleen and tried to push her. Kathleen darted out of her way and kicked out, knocking Ronnie off balance. "Way to go, Kathleen!" cheered Desdemona.

Ronnie grabbed for Kathleen's leg and caught hold. Kathleen crouched and tumbled into a forward roll. Ronnie let go, surprised.

"Ha, ha, *ha!*" Sylvie teased Ronnie, sticking out her tongue.

"Let her have it, Kathleen!" called Annie.

"Had enough?" Kathleen asked Ronnie.

The large girl still looked confused.

Suddenly Ronnie leapt up, her arms stretched out to grab Kathleen. Quick as a flash, Kathleen tossed Ronnie over her shoulder. Then she turned, ready for Ronnie's next attack.

"Get her, guys!" Ronnie screamed.

Kathleen looked over her shoulder. Cheryl and Jodi were running toward her.

"Hey, no fair!" Desdemona shouted.

Cheryl threw herself at Kathleen, her stringy black hair flying behind her. Kathleen ducked. Just as Cheryl sailed into her back, Kathleen arched, bouncing Cheryl off and onto the ground.

In a split second, Jodi was on her, grabbing at Kathleen's hair. With a stiff arm, Kathleen blocked Jodi. Then, with a quick kick to the legs, Kathleen knocked Jodi off her feet.

Jodi flipped backward as if someone had pulled a chair out from under her.

"All right! Way to go!" cried Sharon.

Kathleen glanced quickly at her new friends. They were huddled together, hopping up and down excitedly and punching the air with their fists. Not one of them looked as if she was about to jump in and help.

Ronnie was on her feet now. With a growl

she swiped out at Kathleen.

But Kathleen was too fast. She dodged every punch. She wished Ronnie would give up, but the tall girl just kept swinging.

Kathleen backed up. "Running away, geek?" Ronnie jeered.

Without answering, Kathleen ran toward Ronnie at full speed. With a single bound, she delivered a flying side kick to Ronnie's shoulder.

Again Ronnie hit the ground with a thud. She clutched her arm as she sat up. "You broke my arm, Stoppelmeyer!" she shouted angrily. Wobbling a bit, she rose to her feet. "I'd cream you if my arm wasn't broken."

Kathleen just stood there, panting. Jodi and Cheryl crowded around Ronnie. "Let's get out of here," Ronnie muttered.

Silently, the DO GOODERS watched the three girls walk off. Then they broke into wild cheers. "Awesome!" Desdemona shouted.

"I was about to help you when Jodi and Cheryl jumped in," said Annie. "But I didn't want to get in your way."

"Me, too," agreed Sharon. "I would have helped, but you didn't seem to need me."

"That's okay," Kathleen said. They were probably right. They might have gotten in her way.

"Do you think you really broke Ronnie's arm?" Sylvie asked.

Kathleen smiled, still catching her breath. She *had* been awesome, she realized happily. "I don't think so," she said. "That Ronnie's just a big baby."

"The first victory for the DO GOODERS club!" Sharon cried.

"DO GOODERS rule!" cheered Annie.

Sylvie and Lori made a chair by clasping each other's wrists. "Climb on," said Sylvie.

With a grin, Kathleen settled herself between their wrists. She balanced with both hands on their slim shoulders and let them carry her along.

"Hurray for Kathleen, the Karate Queen!" Annie shouted.

"Kathleen! Kathleen, Karate Queen!" the others picked up the chant. They sang it over and over as Kathleen bobbed along on her human chair.

"Hurray for Kathleen!"

Suddenly Lori stumbled, falling into Sylvie. Kathleen felt herself slide as Lori and Sylvie tumbled to the ground. She fell between them, laughing. Soon everyone else was laughing, too.

Kathleen couldn't remember feeling this happy in a long, long time.

6

"Meet me at the Zombie House," Annie told Kathleen over the phone.

It was Saturday afternoon. Back in Cross Corners, Kathleen's Saturdays had always been busy with friends. But nobody in Parkside had ever called Kathleen at home before.

Kathleen was sure she'd heard Annie wrong. "What did you say?" she asked.

"The Zombie House. It's this beat-up old gazebo at the north end of the park. John Jerome and I used to play there when we were little kids. It was so spooky we'd pretend zombies lived there."

Kathleen looked down the hall to see if anyone was listening. "Isn't the north end dangerous?" she whispered.

"Not to us DO GOODERS," Annie said. "Besides, this is an emergency club meeting. I'll wait for you on the corner of Grant

Avenue and Willow, okay?"

"Okay," Kathleen agreed. "I'll meet you in ten minutes."

"See ya then," said Annie.

As Kathleen hung up the phone, there was a knock on the front door. She pulled it open. Aunt Jessie was leaning against the hallway wall.

"Hi, Kath," she said as she came in. "What did you forget to do?"

"What?" Kathleen asked blankly.

"You forgot to look through the peek hole before you answered the door," said Aunt Jessie. "This isn't Cross Corners anymore. You can't open the door to just anyone. You have to be more careful."

Kathleen knew she'd never get used to all the safety precautions they had to take in the city. It had taken her weeks to remember to lock the door behind her when she came in.

For the zillionth time she wished they'd all move back home to Cross Corners. She imagined her father saying, "All right, everyone. Pack your things. We're going home." She'd played the scene over and over in her mind until it seemed almost real.

Kathleen's mother came out of the kitchen with a dish towel in her hands. "Hi, Jessie," she greeted her sister. "Kathleen, who were you talking to on the phone?"

"A friend from school," Kathleen replied.

Aunt Jessie smiled. "I thought you didn't have any friends."

"This is a new friend," said Kathleen. She turned to her mother. "Mama, I'm going to go out for a little while, okay?"

"No, it's not okay," said her mother. "Where exactly is out?"

"Some kids from school are meeting at Harry Park."

"To do what?"

Kathleen thought quickly. Her mother would not approve of her being president of a fighting club, even one named DO GOOD-ERS.

And if she said they were just hanging out, she wouldn't be allowed to go. Kathleen's mother didn't believe hanging out was a real activity. She had never even let the boys hang out with their friends at the Dairy Queen up the road from the farm.

"We're playing soccer," Kathleen lied. Kids played soccer in the park a lot. It was a believable story.

"Did you finish your chores?" her mother asked.

"Can't I do them when I come back?"

"You know very well they're to be done Saturday morning."

"Oh, come on, Ellie," said Aunt Jessie. "It's a beautiful Saturday. Let her go see her friends."

Mrs. Stoppelmeyer scowled at her younger sister. "She can go out after her chores."

"What does she have to do?" Aunt Jessie asked.

"Vacuum, dust, and clean the bathroom," Kathleen mumbled.

"I'll do that for her," said Aunt Jessie. "Since I'm unemployed, I might as well do *something* useful."

"Kathleen's chores are her responsibility," said Mrs. Stoppelmeyer.

"Give the kid a break, Ellie," Aunt Jessie pleaded. "She hasn't had much fun lately."

Mrs. Stoppelmeyer's face softened a bit. "All right, Jessie," she said with a sigh. "But Kathleen, you have to do your chores when you get back. Is that understood?"

"Yes, Mama." Kathleen hugged her aunt. "Thank you, thank you, thank you!" Then she grabbed her jacket from the hook in the hall and headed out the door.

"Be home before supper," Mrs. Stoppelmeyer called after her.

"I will," Kathleen shouted back.

Outside it was a clear, cool day with fat white clouds rolling in the sky. Kathleen ran up Willow Street to Grant Avenue. She got to the corner in time to see Annie hurrying toward her. The expression on her face was serious.

"What's going on?" Kathleen asked Annie when she reached the corner.

Annie took Kathleen by the arm and kept walking. "This is our first official assignment as DO GOODERS."

"What did Ronnie do now?" Kathleen asked.

"It's not Ronnie this time," said Annie. "Rosa's little sister, Lucy, is in trouble. She stood up to some kids who were picking on a first-grader. Now those kids are saying they're going to get her."

"How old are they?" Kathleen asked as she and Annie entered the park.

"They're fourth-graders," said Annie. "And they're real rough kids. Lucy is only in the second grade."

"Fourth-grade kids are picking on first- and second-graders?" Kathleen asked.

"Isn't that low?" said Annie. "Anyway, it happened on Friday. This morning those jerks were outside Rosa's house, waiting for Lucy to come out. Her brothers chased them away, but then they called up and said they were going to get Lucy real good. The poor little girl is terrified."

"Maybe Mr. and Mrs. Santiago should handle it," Kathleen suggested.

"No," Annie said, shaking her head. "This is exactly the kind of thing the DO GOOD-ERS club was formed to take care of. This is our first real mission."

"What about the other day?" Kathleen asked. She was still proud of the way she'd beaten Ronnie. For the rest of the week at school, Ronnie hadn't bothered anyone, even Kathleen.

"That was sort of a surprise test," said Annie. "This is our first actual mission with a planning meeting and everything."

"Oh," Kathleen said. "I guess that makes sense."

They stopped when they reached a thick wooded area. Kathleen thought it looked very dark and scary.

"Come on," said Annie. She headed toward a dirt path that led into the trees.

Kathleen caught her arm. "Are you sure it's safe?" she asked.

"As long as you're here, we're safe," said Annie.

"I don't know," Kathleen said hesitantly.

"What about those wild dogs that chased you and John when you were in the north end a few weeks ago?"

"Oh, I just made that up," said Annie. "I needed an excuse to get a late pass in the office. Then I had to tell the same story to Cracked-in-the-Head. You know how she is about lateness."

"Tell me about it," said Kathleen glumly.

"That's right," Annie said with a smile. "You're always late, too. But you know what? After I made up that story, I heard that there really *are* packs of wild dogs in the park."

"Really?" Kathleen gasped.

"Oh, I don't know," Annie said with a shrug. "I've never seen any."

Just as they started down the dark path, Kathleen heard a voice calling their names. She turned and saw Sharon Fuller huffing and puffing her way across the field toward them. "Hey, wait up!" she called.

Kathleen stopped walking. The beautiful day was turning gray. The wind was picking up, too.

"Hurry up, Sharon," Annie shouted, sounding annoyed. "Sharon is a real pain sometimes," she said to Kathleen. "I never used to like her at all. But she heard Rosa and me talking about forming the DO GOOD-

ERS club and she got all excited about it. What could we say? We didn't want to hurt her feelings. She's not that bad once you get used to her."

Sharon caught up to them then and stopped to get her breath. "I'm so glad I saw you," she panted. "I wasn't about to go into those woods by myself. There are muggers and crazy people in there, you know."

Kathleen looked at Annie. Annie shrugged. "Maybe, but I've never seen any. Besides, the karate queen is with us."

"Does karate really work?" Sharon asked. "I mean, against muggers and crazy people?"

"I don't know," Kathleen admitted. "I never fought anybody like that. Before I came here to Parkside I only had fights with other karate students. And those were class exercises, not real fights."

"If you can fight Ronnie Smith, you're tough enough to fight anybody," said Annie. "Now, come on, you guys."

Kathleen followed her into the woods. Sharon was right behind them. At first the path was spotted with the wavery dull light that came through the thick trees. As they got deeper into the forest, the splotches of light disappeared. It looked more like twilight than morning.

"I don't like this," Sharon said with a shiver.

"It's like in *The Wizard of Oz* when they go through the woods saying, 'Lions and tigers and bears, oh my!'" Annie said.

The girls linked arms and began chanting the line as they went through the woods. Kathleen found that it did make her feel a little less scared about every shadow.

Finally Kathleen caught a glimpse of something white through the dark trees. As they got closer, she saw it was a small white building. It looked like a porch without a house attached to it.

It was easy to see that the gazebo had once been a lovely building. But it obviously hadn't been fixed up in years. The paint was chipped and the whole thing leaned to one side. Some of the wooden slats were broken.

Desdemona waved to them from the edge of the platform. "Hey, you guys!"

"Hey!" Annie shouted to her.

When they reached the Zombie House, Kathleen saw that Sylvie, Sasha, Lori, and Rosa were already there, too. A clap of thunder rumbled overhead.

"It's creepy here," Lori complained. "Why didn't we meet somewhere else?"

"Let's go," said Sylvie, hugging herself

tightly. "I'm really scared."

"A secret club needs a secret clubhouse," said Annie. "Besides, we're perfectly safe. Kathleen is here, remember?"

Just then a flash of lightning lit the woods around them. Sharon screamed. Lori and Sasha clung to one another. Sylvie turned pale.

When the flash was gone, the woods seemed even darker than before. Kathleen heard the patter of raindrops on the trees above them, though only a few made it through the leaves to the ground.

"Did you hear something?" Sylvie asked suddenly.

Kathleen listened. She *did* hear something, a kind of scuffling sound. Then she heard a low growl.

"I heard it, too," Sharon said with a shiver.

"Me, too," added Annie.

"Let's run for it," Lori suggested.

"No," said Desdemona. "If we run, whoever—or whatever—that is out there might chase us. Kathleen, you'd better go check it out."

"Me?" Kathleen gasped.

"Well, you *are* the president of the club," said Sharon.

"Yes, but..." Kathleen didn't know what to

say. Then she remembered how her friends had carried her, chanting, "Kathleen! Kathleen, Karate Queen!" She didn't want them to think she was a coward now.

Maybe the sound was just dogs, anyway. Kathleen's family had had five dogs on the farm. Four German shepherds and a sheepdog named Dotty. But what if these were the wild dogs? Were wild dogs like wolves?

The growl came again, louder this time.

"Are you going, Kathleen?" Sylvie asked. Her voice was trembling with fear.

"Oh, all right," Kathleen agreed reluctantly. What else could she do? Her friends were all expecting her to do *something*.

Kathleen walked down the broken steps and back through the woods. She heard the low growl again. It seemed to be coming from the bottom of a steep hill behind the gazebo.

Another clap of thunder pounded in her ears. Maybe she could just run away. No, she had to be brave. That's what everyone expected of her.

Crouching low, Kathleen darted from tree to tree. The noise was getting louder now.

What if it wasn't a dog at all? Could it be a crazy person? A murderer lying in wait for a victim? A zombie?

Again, a flash of lightning lit the woods.

Then Kathleen saw them. Two large dogs had torn open a black plastic garbage bag. They were rummaging through it. Every once in a while, they growled at one another over the same piece of garbage.

From behind a tree, Kathleen picked up a large rock. "Get out of here!" she shouted. Then she hurled the rock at a tree high above the dogs.

The dogs jumped back, their ears perked up straight. "Go! Scat!" Kathleen shouted the way she had at the dogs on the farm when they tried to get into the chicken yard. The dogs bounded off into the woods.

"Kathleen!" she heard Annie shout from somewhere behind her. "Are you all right?"

Kathleen was about to call back to her, but then she changed her mind.

This was her big chance to really impress the DO GOODERS.

Quickly she reached down and wiped her hands in the dirt. She smeared it on her face and hands. Then she pulled out her hair elastic and mussed her hair. "And don't come back!" she shouted at no one.

"Kathleen!" Annie cried again.

Kathleen walked back to the top of the embankment. Her friends were running down the path toward her. Annie was in the lead. "She's okay!" Annie shouted to the others.

Kathleen staggered up the path toward them. "It was horrible," she said. "There was a whole pack of wild dogs. They had horrible fangs, and they kept coming at me. I hit their leader with a flying spin kick. I hated to do it, but he would have torn me to shreds. The other dogs ran when they saw the pack leader go down."

"Oh, how awful!" cried Sasha.

"And," Kathleen added dramatically, "I think one of them was carrying a hand."

"A *hand*?" Rosa cried. She looked as though she was about to faint.

Kathleen nodded gravely. "I guess those dogs had already attacked some other poor person already. They got his hand. Who knows what else they got?"

"Those dogs could have killed us!" Sharon sobbed.

"You saved our lives, Kathleen," Annie said.

"Yes," Kathleen agreed. "I guess I did."

7

"There they are," said Rosa. She pointed to a bunch of kids hanging around the far end of the duck pond. "Those are the ones who have been bothering Lucy. They always hang out by the pond there."

"Come on," said Kathleen, leading the way. Since she'd led the other DO GOODERS out of the dark woods, Kathleen had felt strong and fierce. She was full of her own power, as if she should be wearing a superhero cape. Who cared about a bunch of wimpy fourth-graders?

A cool, damp breeze touched her cheeks like fingers. The storm had blown through quickly, but the sky was still dark with thunderclouds.

"Yo!" Annie shouted at the three boys and two girls who were sitting near the pond. At the sound of her voice, the brown duck swimming in the pond and her three ducklings swam quickly to the far side of the pond.

The kids looked up and gazed at the girls. The largest boy wore ripped denim jeans. His shaggy hair curled around the collar of his denim jacket. The other boys wore dirty T-shirts and jeans. The three girls wore jeans and T-shirts, too. Their hair was long and messy.

"Are you the kids who've been bugging Lucy Santiago?" Annie challenged.

The large boy in the jacket stood up. "What's it to you?"

"Lucy Santiago is a friend of ours," said Annie.

"And she's my sister," added Rosa, sounding bolder than usual.

"Big deal," said the boy. His friends gathered around him.

"If you bother Lucy again, *we're* going to bother *you*," said Desdemona.

"Yeah," Sylvie added.

The boy held out his hands and pretended to tremble. "Like I'm really scared of a bunch of girls. Look at me, I'm shaking." His friends snickered.

"You'd shake if you knew what we meant," said Annie. "We're not kidding around."

"Buzz off," said the boy.

"What's your name?" Kathleen asked, stepping forward.

"You can call me Mad Dog," said the boy, folding his arms.

Annie laughed scornfully. "Oh, give me a break. I know your name. It's Harold Kelly."

"Listen, Harold," Kathleen began.

"Don't call me that!" Harold snapped angrily. Kathleen got the idea that calling this kid Harold was the same as calling Ronnie Smith Veronica.

"Okay, Mad Dog," Kathleen went on. "All we want is for you to stop picking on Rosa's sister."

The boy shrugged. "And what if I don't?"

"Then she'll just have to cream you," said Annie.

"Who's going to cream me?" Harold–Mad Dog sneered.

"*She* will!" said all the girls at once. They pointed straight at Kathleen.

"Don't make me laugh," said Mad Dog. "That little squirt?"

Everyone was staring at Kathleen. She had to stay tough now. "Yeah, me," she said, assuming a karate stance.

"Oh, so you want to fight," Mad Dog jeered. "Well, come on. This should be over in about half a second."

Kathleen took another step forward. She didn't really want to fight. Karate was supposed to be for self-defense. But her new friends were depending on her now. She wasn't quiet Kathleen Stoppelmeyer now. She was Kathleen, Karate Queen!

Mad Dog lifted his fists and began to dance around. Kathleen breathed deeply and paid close attention to his every move, just as Mr. Funakoshi had taught her. When the boy jabbed with his right fist, she darted out of the way. Then, with lightning speed, she kicked out and scooped his legs out from under him.

The other boys laughed as Harold–Mad Dog landed in the wet grass. "Anybody else want to fight?" Kathleen challenged.

None of the fourth-graders came forward.

"If anyone messes with Lucy Santiago, they'll get more of the same," Kathleen threatened.

"Believe it!" added Sylvie.

Feeling triumphant, Kathleen turned to join her friends. But in the next second, something hit Kathleen's back with a thud, knocking the breath out of her. Harold–Mad Dog had jumped up and tackled her! She staggered under the boy's weight. For a moment, Kathleen was afraid she would lose her balance and fall to the ground.

She staggered forward with the boy's arms wrapped around her shoulders. Determined not to fall, Kathleen grabbed the boy's arms. Then, with all her strength, she pushed up, breaking his hold. *"Eeeeeeeee-iiiii-yaahhhhh!"* she shouted as she curved her back and rolled Harold—Mad Dog over her shoulder.

"Uuugh!" the boy grunted as he hit the ground again.

"You flipped him right over!" Desdemona cried in amazement.

The fourth-grade kids backed up, leaving Harold—Mad Dog grazing in the grass.

Kathleen rubbed her right shoulder. It hurt all the way up to her neck.

"All right, Kathleen!" Annie cheered. She moved toward the group of fourth-graders and they stepped back again. "Remember the DO GOODERS club and Kathleen, Karate Queen. Tell your friends that if you want to mess with the helpless, we'll be there!"

On Annie's signal all the club members turned and walked away. When they were several paces from Mad Dog and his friends, Desdemona leaped high and punched the air. "First mission accomplished!" she shouted.

The girls linked arms and continued across the park. Together they walked out of the park and onto Grant Avenue. Then Rosa, Sharon, and Lori, turned off on the next street. "I'll tell Lucy she doesn't have to worry anymore," Rosa called as she waved good-bye. "Thanks, everybody. Thanks, Kathleen."

"You're welcome," Kathleen said, waving back.

Sasha lived on Grant. Annie, Sylvie, and Desdemona walked down Willow with Kathleen. "I'm going to the Pathway to see my mother," said Annie. "She works in the office there. Anyone want to come? Sometimes she treats me and my friends to a soda or something."

"Okay," said Sylvie.

"Sure," agreed Desdemona.

"I'd better not," said Kathleen, rubbing her neck. "I should go home and do my chores."

"Too bad," said Annie. "You know, I wish we'd gotten to know you sooner. We could have solved a lot of problems. You know, Ronnie hasn't bugged anyone all week."

"That's true," said Desdemona. "Keep up the good work, Kathleen."

"We should have been nicer to you a long

time ago," said Sylvie. "But we thought you were so quiet and all."

Kathleen felt embarrassed. "Everybody seemed to have friends already," she said. "Back in Cross Corners I knew all the kids from the time I was a baby. But here I felt funny just walking up to kids I didn't know and saying hi. I'd never had to do that before."

"Well, we're friends now," said Desdemona, putting her hand on Kathleen's shoulder. Kathleen winced with pain.

Annie gave her a pat on the back. "You'd better go home and rest. I mean, you've just fought a pack of dogs in the woods and a mean little punk. Are you okay?"

"I pulled my shoulder, but it'll be okay." Kathleen felt warm all over. It was great to have friends.

"Do you think we should tell the police about those dogs in the woods?" Sylvie asked.

"Nah," said Annie. "The north end's probably full of them. I didn't believe it at first, but I guess it's true. Maybe we should find a new clubhouse."

"Good idea," agreed Sylvie.

Kathleen was glad they'd decided not to call the police. What a mess *that* would have been! She wasn't sure why she'd told everyone that story. Was she afraid they wouldn't like her as much if she wasn't a fearless karate queen? Maybe. But she didn't want to think about that.

Annie, Desdemona, and Sylvie said good-bye to Kathleen in front of her apartment house, then continued down the street. As she opened the iron gate that led to the front yard, Kathleen saw Aunt Jessie walking out of the house. Her wild blond hair was up in a tight bun. She was wearing a blue business suit. "Hi, Kath," she said. She sounded very distracted. Luckily, she didn't seem to notice the dirt on Kathleen's clothes and her messed-up hair.

"I came back to finish my chores," Kathleen told her.

Aunt Jessie gave her a small smile. "Great. Wish me luck. I have a job interview."

"On Saturday?" Kathleen asked.

Aunt Jessie nodded. "It's for a job as a receptionist at a dog grooming place."

Kathleen nodded. "At least you'll be around animals."

Aunt Jessie laughed grimly. "That's looking on the bright side, I guess."

"Well, good luck," said Kathleen.

Aunt Jessie looked at Kathleen and frowned. "Your cheek is scratched," she said.

Kathleen's hand flew to her face. Suddenly she remembered Harold–Mad Dog's nails brushing past her face when she flipped him. "You should see the other guy," she joked.

Aunt Jessie gasped. "You've been fighting? Kath, what happened? Was someone bothering you?"

"No, " Kathleen said. "Everything's okay."

"Are you sure?" Aunt Jessie pressed.

"Yes," Kathleen assured her. "Really."

Aunt Jessie glanced at her watch. Then she gazed down Willow Street. "This city is a crazy place," she said. "I don't know how people live here."

Kathleen's spirits lifted. Aunt Jessie still wanted to leave! But did she still want to go with Aunt Jessie? She wasn't sure anymore. Back in Cross Corners she'd just be Kathleen Stoppelmeyer again. Here, in Parkside, she was Kathleen, Karate Queen.

"Do you still want to go back to Cross Corners?" Aunt Jessie asked.

"Sure," Kathleen replied, even though she wasn't.

"If I get this job, I'll keep it just long enough to make the money to get out of here," Aunt Jessie said.

"Good luck," Kathleen said again.

"Thanks," Aunt Jessie said. Kathleen watched her go through the gate and down the street. She looked all wrong in that suit. And her broad, strong shoulders were hunched. City life was beating Aunt Jessie. Kathleen had always thought nothing or no one could ever do that.

When she got upstairs, the apartment was quiet. "Mama?" Kathleen called.

"I'm in the kitchen," her mother called back. There was something strange and choked about her voice. Kathleen hurried down the hall. Her mother was sitting at the kitchen table with her forehead against her hand.

"Are you sick?" Kathleen asked quickly.

When her mother turned toward her, Kathleen saw that her eyes were red and puffy, as if she'd been crying. In all her life, Kathleen had never seen her mother cry.

"Don't mind me," Mrs. Stoppelmeyer said with a wave of her hand. "It's just this silly magazine job. It's hard to be hung up on five times in a row. And your father's working so hard, and the farm is gone forever and—" Her mother made a fist and held it to her mouth. She gazed at the ceiling for a moment until her expression grew calmer. Then the usual stern look came back to her face.

She looked sharply at Kathleen. "Your jacket is ripped," she said.

Kathleen fingered the flap of red cloth that hung from her elbow. It was the tear that had happened at the beginning of the week when Ronnie stumbled into her. "I fell in the schoolyard," she told her mother.

Mrs. Stoppelmeyer got up and examined the jacket. "Take this off," she ordered. "I'll have to patch it. You know, when I was a girl we had no money, but we always looked presentable. That's very important."

Kathleen shrugged off the jacket and handed it to her mother.

"I wish you'd be more careful with your clothes," Mrs. Stoppelmeyer went on. "We have to make everything last until we get on our feet again." She glanced back at Kathleen. "What happened to your face?"

"A branch scratched it," Kathleen said.

Mrs. Stoppelmeyer's eyes narrowed. "You weren't fighting, were you?"

Kathleen shook her head.

Mrs. Stoppelmeyer looked at Kathleen as if she didn't believe her. "Are you sure?"

"Yes," Kathleen lied.

Her mother still didn't look convinced. "You know, I never liked you taking those karate lessons. I thought it would get you into situations you couldn't handle. You're very small, you know."

"I know, Mama," Kathleen said.

Mrs. Stoppelmeyer shook her head wearily as she studied the ripped jacket. "There are a lot of things we can't afford anymore that I'm sorry about. But not those karate lessons. I was always worried that you'd wind up hurt."

"Mama, I'm okay," Kathleen said. She wished her mother would stop talking like this. She was making her feel like a baby. Kathleen wanted to keep thinking of herself as a karate queen. Her mother wasn't making it easy.

"Get me my sewing box from the living room closet," said Mrs. Stoppelmeyer.

Kathleen headed to the living room and got the box. As she passed the windows, she stopped to gaze down at the busy street. Somewhere, as usual, a siren was blaring. Dirty-looking pigeons bobbed around on the rooftop across the way. Someone's car alarm suddenly went off, drowning out the siren.

Kathleen looked down at her father's old blue Buick and froze. Someone was leaning up against it. The person lifted her chin and looked up at Kathleen's window. It was Ronnie Smith.

8

Kathleen stood nervously in the lobby of her building, hoping her mother wouldn't realize she had left the apartment. Had Ronnie heard about the DO GOODERS? Was she a friend of Harold–Mad Dog Kelly? Had she come here for revenge?

There was only one way to find out. Obviously, Ronnie was waiting for Kathleen. Kathleen knew she had to show her she wasn't frightened. Gathering her courage, she pushed open the front door.

When Ronnie saw her, she got off the car, whose alarm continued to blare. *Even the car knows she's bad news,* thought Kathleen, walking toward her.

As Kathleen got closer, she noticed something odd about Ronnie. She was smiling! Ronnie didn't look quite right with a smile on her face—as if her face wasn't used it.

The smile threw Kathleen off. She didn't know what to say.

"I looked up your address in the phone book," Ronnie said. "Man! Your last name is hard to spell."

"You've been waiting for me?" Kathleen asked.

"Yeah. I got to talk to you about something," Ronnie said.

"Like what?" Kathleen hoped she sounded cool.

"Um, you want to take a walk? We can talk about it then."

What was going on? Was Ronnie leading her into a trap? Were Cheryl and Jodi waiting around the corner?

"I don't know," said Kathleen.

Ronnie gave her a sneering smile this time. "Is the karate queen scared?"

"I'm not scared," Kathleen said. "I just don't know why we can't talk here."

"I talk better when I'm walking," said Ronnie. "Besides, I want to talk to you alone. I don't want any of your geeky friends coming around."

Kathleen didn't really want to be seen chatting with Ronnie Smith, either. She glanced up at the windows of her apartment. Her mother was still working on her jacket, but the day had gotten a bit warmer. She could skip the jacket. Folding her arms against the breeze, Kathleen nodded. "Okay."

"Let's go to Ice Cream Heaven," Ronnie suggested. "My treat."

Kathleen imagined Ronnie holding some poor kid upside down and shaking the change out of his pocket. "No thanks," she said.

"Okay. But if you change your mind, let me know," said Ronnie.

The two of them started walking up Willow Street. They walked past three buildings without speaking. Kathleen felt strange to be walking beside Ronnie Smith.

"Here's the thing," Ronnie said finally. "Maybe I've been kind of hard on you. I mean, it wasn't your fault that jerk John Jerome pushed me into you. And that's where our problems started, right?"

"I guess so," Kathleen said.

"So what I'm trying to say is, you and me should be friends," Ronnie said.

Friends! With *Ronnie Smith?*

Kathleen couldn't believe it. This was too weird for words.

"A lot of kids don't really like me," Ronnie went on. "I know that. But I think they're jealous of me."

"You do?" Kathleen asked.

"Yeah. Because, you know, I've got my own gang. And I don't need nobody else. I'm a leader."

Me too, Kathleen thought proudly. She decided not to tell Ronnie about the DO GOODERS club, though.

"Well, you're the leader type, too," Ronnie went on as if she'd been reading Kathleen's mind. "I see the way the other kids hang around you now."

It was strange to be chatting with someone she'd dumped on the ground the last time they were together. "I hope I didn't hurt you," Kathleen said, feeling ridiculous even as she spoke.

"Nah, I can take it," said Ronnie. "Forget about it." The way Ronnie talked, the words came out sounding like *Fah-ged-aboud-id.*

"Do you live around here?" Kathleen asked, trying to be polite.

"Sort of," said Ronnie. "I live just off Harrison South, by the cemetery. It's not all fancy like around here."

Kathleen knew Ronnie had that wrong. Her block wasn't fancy at all.

"My family isn't rich," Kathleen pointed out as they reached Grant Avenue.

"I can tell," said Ronnie, nodding. "You're not all stuck up."

"I'm not really even from Parkside. I grew up on a farm."

"See!" said Ronnie. "I knew it! You're not like those other kids at school. I said to Jodi just yesterday, 'Kathleen's not from Parkside. She's got to be from somewheres else.' You can ask Jodi. I really said that."

"Well, I moved here in June," Kathleen said.

"I remember you from last year," Ronnie said. "You was real quiet. Not like those rich snots."

Kathleen was a bit flattered that Ronnie had noticed her. Maybe everyone misjudged Ronnie. Once you got to know her, she wasn't so bad. The only problem was that the kids Ronnie noticed usually ended up getting hurt.

"Is that why you're always fighting?" Kathleen asked. "Because you think the rich kids look down on you?"

"Nobody looks down on me!" Ronnie said angrily. Her scarred lip twitched. "I told you, it's 'cause they're jealous. See, I don't have money, but I have respect. People respect me and that makes kids jealous."

Kathleen's head spun as she tried to keep

up with Ronnie's reasoning.

"I didn't mean to insult you," Kathleen said honestly. "I was just trying to understand."

Ronnie thumped Kathleen's bruised shoulder with her heavy hand. "No problem. Listen, how about I call you Katie?"

"No one ever has," Kathleen replied. "But I've always kind of liked that name, I guess."

"See?" Ronnie cried happily. "I can tell stuff like that about you. Okay, Katie, how about I buy you an ice cream? That's the least I can do after the hard time I've been giving you."

"All right," Kathleen agreed. They walked into Ice Cream Heaven with its deep pink walls and small, round marble-top tables. "A Rocky Road cone, please," Kathleen told the teenage girl behind the counter.

"Me, too!" cried Ronnie. "Rocky Road is my best flavor. No kidding."

They sat at a table and ate their cones. Kathleen wondered what anyone would think if they saw her having ice cream with Ronnie Smith. What if one of the DO GOODERS happened to come in right then?

They finished and went outside. "Come here a minute, Katie," said Ronnie. She waved for Kathleen to follow her down the alley between Ice Cream Heaven and the Music Corner.

In back of the music store was a cement patio cluttered with empty cardboard boxes. An orange tiger-striped cat ran out of the yard as they approached. Ronnie leaned up against the building and pulled a crumpled pack of cigarettes from her jeans pocket. "I've been dying for a butt all day," she said, taking a cigarette from the pack.

"You *smoke*?" Kathleen gasped.

"Sure," said Ronnie, lighting up. "I have to do it back here, though. If my mother went by and saw me, I'd catch a beating. She smokes like a house on fire, but she caught me smoking once and, man, did I get it."

Ronnie held the pack out to Kathleen.

"No, thanks," Kathleen said.

Ronnie snorted. "What, are you afraid of getting lung cancer?"

"Yes," Kathleen said.

"One crummy little butt isn't going to make you sick," Ronnie said, as smoke poured out her nose. She stuck another cigarette in her mouth and lit it. Then she handed it to Kathleen.

Kathleen shrank back. She knew smoking was terrible for her health. But she was curious, too. What did a cigarette taste like?

She took the burning cigarette from Ronnie. But just holding it made her eyes water. And she hated the disgusting smell. "No thanks," she said, handing the cigarette back to Ronnie.

"Okay, suit yourself," said Ronnie, throwing the smoking cigarette onto the ground. "I'm glad you and me are friends now. With you in my gang, we can really clobber those Parkside snots."

The smoke from Ronnie's cigarette was starting to make Kathleen cough. "What do you mean, clobber the Parkside kids?"

"I mean, with your karate know-how on my side, we'll be unbeatable. Me and you'll be a team, with Cheryl and Jodi for backup, of course."

Kathleen's mouth dropped open. "You want me to *fight* for you? So that's why you came around today."

"No, we're friends now," Ronnie said.

"You're not my friend," Kathleen said. "You just want me to be a...a secret weapon!"

"You're crazy, man," Ronnie snapped. She looked like her old, nasty self again.

"I'm not crazy," Kathleen said. She began walking back up the alley. "And there's no way I'm going to be your secret weapon."

Ronnie stepped out into the alley. "That's

the only reason your new friends like you," she called after Kathleen. "That's all you are to them. A stupid old secret weapon!"

Kathleen's shoulders shot up. It was as if Ronnie's words were a knife. And she'd thrown it straight into Kathleen's back.

The weekend was very long.

Kathleen's mother seemed quiet and sad, as if there was something on her mind. Kathleen's father came in late Saturday night and slept nearly all of Sunday. Her brothers were out most of the time.

On Sunday, Kathleen thought of calling Annie. But for some reason, Kathleen felt funny about calling her. Besides, her shoulder had grown stiff and painful. Maybe it would be best to just stay home.

Aunt Jessie came up later. In her jeans and faded blue T-shirt she looked much more like herself than she had in the blue suit. "How did your job interview go yesterday?" Kathleen asked.

"Terrible," said Aunt Jessie. She plunked herself down on the green checked couch in the living room. "I didn't like the woman there. And she didn't like me much, either."

"That's too bad," said Kathleen.

"It wasn't a great job anyway." Aunt Jessie sighed. "I guess it would have paid the bills, though." Aunt Jessie pushed her hair off her face with two hands.

"It's too bad you can't teach karate here," Kathleen said.

"That'd be great," Aunt Jessie agreed. "But I haven't really been practicing since we moved here. And I've never taught before."

"You've helped me with my karate," Kathleen reminded her. "And you've taught me how to do gymnastics. You're a great teacher."

"Thanks," said Aunt Jessie. "Imagine me teaching. Wouldn't Mr. Funakoshi be surprised?"

Kathleen sat beside Aunt Jessie on the couch. "I miss Mr. Funakoshi," she said.

"Me too," Aunt Jessie said. "He always seemed to have a lot of inner peace. He'd say, 'Fight only in self-defense. To cause a fight is the coward's way.' When he talked like that it made you wonder why anyone would ever fight at all."

That night Kathleen dreamed about fighting. Her dream had no real story. But it was full of faces and fights. She saw herself kicking and leaping through the air, at Ronnie Smith and Harold–Mad Dog Kelly.

In her dream, Harold–Mad Dog turned into the two snarling dogs she'd seen in the park. Then, right before her eyes, the dogs changed. They melted together and turned into Dotty the sheepdog. Suddenly she was running through a field with the shaggy dog. She was throwing a stick for her and laughing. Suddenly, the earth below her feet began to shake. Then it began to split. Dotty was slipping into the deep crack in the ground. Kathleen tried to catch her, but the terrified dog slipped out of her grip.

Kathleen's eyes snapped open. In her dark room, she lay very still, not quite sure where she was. Her heart was pounding.

She sat up slowly. A sharp ray of light from the streetlight cut across her bed. Somewhere, out in the dark night, a siren blared. Then Kathleen remembered she was no longer in Cross Corners.

The next morning, Kathleen felt as if she hadn't slept at all. But even though she was tired she got to school on time. Somehow Harry Park didn't hold its same charm that morning. It didn't make her want to do a forward flip in the air. It just seemed like a place where she might have to fight someone.

In the schoolyard, the DO GOODERS stood together in a group. John Jerome and

Carlos Ortega were with them. "Big news," Sharon said when Kathleen joined them. "Carlos and John have joined the DO GOOD-ERS."

John and Carlos were okay. But Kathleen didn't like the idea of boys in the club. She wasn't sure why. Maybe it was because her brothers and their friends always tried to run things.

"I thought we were going to vote on new members," Kathleen said to the girls in a low voice.

"We did vote," said Sharon. "And we all voted yes. So even if you'd been here and voted no, you'd still have been outvoted."

"And since you're always late, we didn't want to wait around for you," added Desdemona.

"We didn't think you'd mind," said Annie.

"Do you?" Sylvie asked.

Kathleen didn't know what to say. She didn't want to hurt the boys' feelings. "I guess not," she said. "I wish you'd waited for me, though."

"Next time we will," said Lori.

"Next time?" Kathleen asked.

"Sure," said John. "This club is the coolest thing around. Everybody's heard about how you creamed Ronnie in the park last week. She's had it coming a long time."

"Yeah, and Harold Kelly deserved it, too. That kid is a real creep," added Carlos.

"Everybody wants to join the club," said Sharon happily. "We're so cool."

"DO GOODERS rule!" cried John, pumping his fist in the air. "We are cool! DO GOODERS rule!"

The other kids picked up the chant. "We are cool! DO GOODERS rule!" They began singing it over and over. But Kathleen couldn't bring herself to join in. She didn't like the idea that they'd made a decision without even asking her. What was the sense of being president when no one even asked her what she thought about things? It made being president sort of meaningless.

Annie gave her a nudge. "Hey, you're the president of the coolest club in school."

Kathleen nodded. "Cool," she echoed flatly.

As the kids chanted, she saw Ronnie, Cheryl, and Jodi standing against the wall watching them.

"Hey, what are you guys looking at?" Carlos called over to them.

"Nothing," Ronnie replied. "I'm looking at a lot of nothing."

"Well, you're the biggest nothing around here," John shot back. He stepped out of the group toward Ronnie.

"Shut up, fat mouth," Ronnie snapped.

"Come over here and say that," John shouted.

Ronnie lifted her chin and started walking toward the group.

A thrilled whisper spread throughout the schoolyard. "Fight! Fight! Fight!" Kathleen heard the other kids saying. They gathered in a wide circle around Ronnie, Cheryl, Jodi, and the DO GOODERS club.

John looked over at Kathleen and grinned. He seemed excited about this fight, not scared at all. He walked right up to Ronnie and stuck his face into hers. Then he jabbed her right shoulder.

With a sneer, Ronnie shoved him to the ground. The smile left John's face. He tried to scramble up, but Ronnie used her foot to push him right back down.

John grabbed her leg. He tried to throw her over backward. But Ronnie shook him off. Then she kicked him, hard, right in the face.

A horrified gasp swept the schoolyard. Blood was running down John's nose. He sat on the ground wiping blood from his face.

Suddenly Kathleen realized that everyone

was looking at her. "Do something, Kathleen!" Sharon hissed.

A group of kids began to chant. "Kathleen, Karate Queen! Kathleen, Karate Queen!"

Kathleen knew what she was expected to do. She was supposed to step forward and knock Ronnie down. She could do it, too.

But Kathleen couldn't get the picture of Mr. Funakoshi out of her head. She kept hearing his words. *"Fight only in self-defense."*

Ronnie hadn't started this fight. John and Carlos had. John hadn't hit Ronnie hard, but he'd jabbed her first. This wasn't self-defense.

Kathleen also knew that Ronnie was weaker than she was. The girl might be really mean, but she wasn't a good fighter. She was clumsy and off balance.

"Kathleen!" Sharon cried urgently.

"Don't just stand there!" Desdemona said in a loud whisper.

Kathleen shook her head slowly. She didn't know what to say. How could she make them understand?

"Ha!" Ronnie snorted with laughter. "I guess that's the end of that." She stepped forward suddenly and the crowd of kids jumped back. "Get outta here!" she shouted. The kids scurried away like ants.

"What's going on here?" demanded Ms. McCracken, hurrying over from the other side of the schoolyard.

Ronnie glared at John.

"He tripped," Sharon spoke up. "Tripped and hit his nose."

Ms. McCracken's red lips tightened into a thin line. She looked at all of them, as if her eyes could see into their heads. "Is that so?" she said. She held her hand out to John firmly. "Come with me, Mr. Jerome. We'll let the nurse have a look at your nose. We can't have you bleeding all over the school."

John left the schoolyard with Ms. McCracken. "Poor John," said Annie.

"I hope his nose is all right," added Sylvie.

The rest of the DO GOODERS stared icily at Kathleen. "I'm sorry," Kathleen began. "I just couldn't...You see—"

"We're disgraced!" Desdemona wailed.

"Disgraced by our own club president," Sharon cried. "Why didn't you help him, Kathleen?"

"I'm trying to tell you—" Kathleen's voice choked as tears came to her eyes.

"Oh, no!" Sharon shouted. "What kind of karate queen *cries*? This is a disaster!"

For the first time ever, Kathleen was glad when Ms. McCracken's class began. At least she wouldn't have to think about how she'd disappointed her ex new friends. She could forget about them and their cold, betrayed looks. She could forget the purple bruise on John's chin, and his swollen nose. Instead she could pay attention to what Ms. McCracken had to say about white blood cells.

Ms. McCracken asked whether anyone knew what purpose white blood cells served. Rosa—who always knew the answer to every science question—stood up. "White blood cells attack germs in the bloodstream," she said. She sounded proud of the white blood cells for doing their job so bravely and well.

Then Ms. McCracken asked whether white blood cells attacked only certain germs. She called on Annie this time. "No," said

Annie, getting to her feet. "They attack anything in the blood that they don't recognize as belonging there. They go right for it and pulverize it. Pow! Whammo! Those white blood cells don't fool around." She glanced at Kathleen. "And they don't stand there doing nothing while another blood cell gets creamed. White blood cells have guts."

"Thank you. You may sit down, Ms. Tuzmarti," said Ms. McCracken sternly.

At lunch, Kathleen didn't know where to sit. She always sat with the DO GOODERS now. She wasn't sure she'd be welcome today, though. Then she noticed that the chair she usually sat on had been shoved over to an empty table. The DO GOODERS kept their backs to her.

Kathleen saw Sylvie sneak a small peek as she went by with her tray. Rosa, too, looked up. But both girls ducked their heads again when their eyes met Kathleen's. Kathleen's heart sunk. If Rosa and Sylvie wouldn't speak to her, the others surely wouldn't.

She'd have to sit by herself once again. And she didn't have a book with her this time.

Kathleen found a seat at the back of the lunchroom. It wasn't easy forcing down the gooey macaroni and cheese. The yellow noodles stuck in her throat like paste.

She didn't know where to look either. No matter which way she turned, someone was staring at her. She finally solved the problem by focusing on the red exit sign at the back of the cafeteria. She stared at it so hard her eyes watered.

After lunch, Kathleen started to feel sick. She ran into the girls' room and threw up. She was still feeling shaky when she came out of the bathroom stall. And to make matters worse, Ronnie was waiting for her.

"Lost your lunch, huh?" Ronnie jeered.

Kathleen shot her a cold look as she washed her hands.

"Looks like you lost all your new pals, too," Ronnie kept on. "What a shame. All alone."

"Shut up," Kathleen snapped. She headed for the door.

Ronnie put her hand on the wall and blocked her path. "You screwed up, Stoppelmeyer. Let's see how tough you are without your little fan club."

"Tough enough," said Kathleen.

"Enough to fight all three of us?"

"Sure," said Kathleen. But she wasn't.

"When you least expect it, we'll find out," Ronnie said. "Count on it." She pushed off the tile wall and slammed out of the bathroom.

Another wave of nausea swept over Kathleen. She went back into the stall and got sick again.

That afternoon, Kathleen didn't want to see anyone. She cut across the Harry Park soccer field and came out onto Harrison South. From there she ducked into the Parkside Cemetery. It would take her an extra fifteen minutes to get home, but she didn't care. It would be worth it to avoid everyone.

Kathleen walked along the cement path that cut past the graves. Suddenly she stopped. Had she heard something snap?

Kathleen sucked in her breath and squared her shoulders. Looking cautiously around, she continued down the path.

Then it happened.

With shrill, warlike cries, Ronnie, Cheryl, and Jodi charged over a low hill. All three of them swung ropes over their heads.

Kathleen started to run. But Ronnie tackled her. They skidded across the cement and onto the grass. Kathleen slammed onto the ground with Ronnie on top of her.

Kathleen squirmed out from under Ronnie and banged her head into a headstone. "Ow!" she cried. She touched her head and felt something warm and wet. When she looked at her hand, she saw blood.

In that stunned moment when Kathleen realized she was bleeding, Cheryl lunged. Kathleen was knocked to the ground again. Before she knew what was happening, Ronnie was tying a rope around her ankles.

Kathleen kicked up, hitting Ronnie in the nose.

Jodi pulled Kathleen's ponytail. Kathleen reached around, grabbed Jodi, and pushed her face into the ground. She jumped to her feet, but her ankles were still tied tight. If she stopped to untie them, one of the girls would surely jump her.

"We've got you now, Stoppelmeyer," Ronnie taunted. "We're going to tie you up, and leave you here all night for the ghosts and the wild dogs."

Kathleen knew they would do it, too. She'd beaten Ronnie in front of everyone. Ronnie would want the worst revenge she could think of. "Someone will find me first," Kathleen said.

Ronnie took a faded red bandanna from her back pocket. "Not if we gag you and stick you behind a big gravestone."

With Jodi's help, Cheryl threw another rope around Kathleen. Kathleen struggled, but with the two of them behind her and her feet tied, it was no use.

Just then, it started to rain. "Looks like you'll be getting a little wet tonight," Ronnie laughed.

Kathleen shivered, and raindrops beat against her face. Maybe the rain would cover the tears she felt welling up. She couldn't bear to cry right now. But, she didn't know if she could help it.

Suddenly Jodi went flying past Kathleen. Kathleen turned her head to see what had happened.

It was Aunt Jessie!

With a spinning back kick Aunt Jessie mowed down Ronnie and Cheryl at the same time. "Why don't you try to tie *me* up, kids?" Aunt Jessie challenged.

Ronnie, Cheryl, and Jodi didn't answer. They jumped up and ran.

Aunt Jessie untied Kathleen. "You're bleeding," she said. "Are you okay?"

Kathleen was crying so hard she couldn't speak.

Aunt Jessie hugged her and held tight while Kathleen cried. "I shouldn't have hit them. I could have just scared them away. But I got so angry when I saw what they were doing to you."

"Thank you," Kathleen whispered through her tears.

Aunt Jessie gave her another hug. "Let's go home," she said. "Your mom will kill me if you catch a cold from being out in the rain."

Kathleen wiped her nose. "Let's really go home, Aunt Jessie," she said, as they started down the path. "To Cross Corners, like we talked about. I want to go now, tonight."

Aunt Jessie sighed. "I can't, Kathleen."

"Why not? You don't have a job yet."

"I just got one. Today."

"But it's a job you'll hate, right? You've hated every job you've had since we got here. Come on, let's go. *Please*?"

Aunt Jessie smiled sadly at Kathleen. "It's a good job, Kath. I'll be teaching beginning karate at the YMCA. They're expanding their martial arts program. If this works out, they might put me in charge of it. It would be the perfect job for me."

Kathleen looked at her aunt through the rain. "That's great. But don't you want to go home? I thought you did! You told me so!"

"I know I did, but things are different now. Besides, I got the feeling that you'd changed your mind. You seemed to be making new friends and all."

Kathleen shook her head. "They're not my friends. They only wanted me for their secret weapon. I can't stay here anymore. I just can't stand it another day."

In the distance, a fire siren blared. Kathleen thought she'd go crazy if she heard one more siren.

"Kath, everything will be okay," said Aunt Jessie gently.

"No it won't!" Kathleen shouted. She ran down the cemetery path, the fire siren ringing in her ears.

11

Kathleen took her getaway money out from under her pillow. Seventeen dollars. She needed twenty.

Her brother Sean walked down the hall. Kathleen shoved her money back under her pillow. "Sean," she called to him.

"What?" he asked, peering into her room.

"Can I borrow three dollars? It's super-important."

"What for?"

"I can't tell you right now. But I swear I'll pay you back, double swear."

"How soon?"

"In a month. Honest."

Sean nodded and left. He came back with three crumpled dollars. "What do you need so badly?" he asked, handing her the money.

"You'll find out by tomorrow. I just can't tell you right now."

Sean looked at her closely. "Are you okay, Kath?"

"I'm fine. Thanks a zillion."

"All right. You have one month. After that I'm charging you extra. That's what banks do, you know."

Kathleen put her hand on his back and guided him out the door. "No problem." She shut the door behind him.

Kathleen pulled her money out again and added the three dollars. Then she rolled all the money up and stuffed it in her front pocket. She put the change into her back pockets, keeping out the subway token she'd found on the street three months ago. She'd need the token to get to the train station.

Kathleen took her backpack out of the closet and threw in an extra pair of jeans, some T-shirts, underwear, and a nightgown. As she packed, she started thinking about where, exactly, she would go once she got to Cross Corners. Maybe Emmy Meyers could sneak her into the guest cottage at the back of her family's property. She could probably survive by collecting cans and newspapers and turning them in to the recycling plant for money. She could walk pets too. She'd done both of those things when she'd lived in Cross Corners before.

Of course, she wouldn't want to be seen. She might get sent back. So she wouldn't be able to go to school. If the teachers saw her they'd want to know where her parents were.

Maybe the Meyerses would take her in. Then when her parents saw how desperate she was to go home, maybe they'd let her stay. Or maybe they'd move back.

The main thing was to get back to Cross Corners. Once she was there, she'd figure out what to do.

Kathleen put her backpack on her shoulders and stuck her head out the door. No one was around. She tiptoed down the hall. In the living room, Adam and Sean were sprawled in front of the TV. Even though her brothers were pains sometimes, she'd miss them.

Martin was on the couch reading *Sports Illustrated*. She'd miss him the most.

Through the paned-glass door to the kitchen she saw her mother on the phone, still trying to sell magazines.

Papa was still at work. She knew her parents would be upset when they discovered she was gone. Kathleen decided she'd write them a note when she got to Cross Corners. She wouldn't tell them where she was, but she'd let them know she was all right.

"Bye, everyone," Kathleen whispered as

she slipped out the door. She'd see them all again—someday.

Just as she got outside, she saw Aunt Jessie coming up the street. She quickly tossed her backpack into a bush in front of the apartment house. "Kath!" Aunt Jessie called.

Kathleen stayed by the door. "Hi," she said, as Aunt Jessie came up.

"Do you feel any better?" Aunt Jessie asked.

Kathleen nodded. She *did* feel better. She was getting away!

"You know, we should call the parents of those girls," said Aunt Jessie. "Do you know them?"

"Yes, but it wouldn't do any good," said Kathleen. "It just makes things worse. Everyone says Ronnie Smith's mother is meaner than she is. And her father isn't around. Ronnie just gets mad and is even meaner to the kid who tells."

"What about the school? Could you tell your teacher?"

"I guess so," said Kathleen. "Even Ronnie is afraid of McCracken."

"I'll call Ms. McCracken if you like," Aunt Jessie volunteered.

"It's okay," said Kathleen. "I'll talk to her tomorrow."

"You're sure?"

"Sure," Kathleen lied. "Listen, I'm going over to Sylvie Levine's house now. I'll see you, and thanks again for helping me in the park."

Aunt Jessie looked puzzled. "I thought you were angry with your friends."

"Um...well, not Sylvie," Kathleen said.

"All right. Have fun," said Aunt Jessie. "I'll talk to you when you get home."

"Okay," said Kathleen. Then she threw her arms around Aunt Jessie and hugged her tightly. "'Bye, Aunt Jessie. I really love you, you know."

Aunt Jessie stroked her hair. "I know you do, Kath. I love you, too."

Kathleen realized Aunt Jessie wasn't going to go inside until she left. She let go of her and, with a wave, she hurried on down the street. Several buildings down, she peeked over her shoulder and saw Aunt Jessie was gone. She ran back, grabbed her pack from behind the bush, and started out again.

The subway ride to the train station seemed very long. Kathleen had never taken the subway before. She'd heard terrible things about it. The subway cars got stuck in the dark tunnels for hours. People were robbed on the subways, too. All Kathleen saw were people who seemed to be coming or going to work. Every so often, a scruffy-looking man would come onto the train and Kathleen would grip her pack a little more tightly. But nothing happened. Finally the subway reached the stop at the train station.

Kathleen followed the crowd into the big, bustling terminal. There were television screens on all the walls showing what trains where going where. They also listed what tracks the trains were on and what time they would be leaving. Kathleen searched a screen for the train to Cross Corners. She couldn't find it.

At the information booth the woman said that there were only two trains a day that stopped at Cross Corners. One left at eleven o'clock in the morning, the other at nine o'clock at night.

"All right, thanks." Kathleen sighed and bought a ticket for the nine o'clock train. Then she took a seat by some men and women dressed in business suits. They took no notice of her at all.

Kathleen wished she had money for a magazine, but she'd spent it all on her ticket.

So she just sat and watched people come and go. There were so many different kinds of people in the city. In Cross Corners, everyone seemed so much alike.

After two hours of sitting and watching, Kathleen's stomach rumbled. Across the waiting room was a snack stand. People were buying hot dogs, pizzas, and sodas. A woman in a red dress gave a raggedy man two dollars. He went to the stand and bought a slice of pizza and a soda. Kathleen's mouth watered as she watched him eat it.

Kathleen put her pack on and went outside. It was much busier in this part of the city than in Parkside. Crowds of people moved quickly in the streets. They reminded Kathleen of herds of sheep going back into the barn from the pasture, only they were moving much faster. The cars were as thick as the people, only they moved slowly down the street, honking their horns. And the sirens were even noisier than in Parkside. Overhead the *chop, chop, chop* of a helicopter blade sounded.

A well-dressed man bit into a hamburger as he walked down the street. In front of the station, he tossed the uneaten part of the hamburger into the trash. Kathleen went to the basket and looked at it. It was probably still good. It was still half in the wrapping.

She reached forward for the uneaten burger, but her hand stopped. She couldn't bring herself to eat from a public trash can. But she was so hungry.

Then Kathleen realized someone else had come to the can. She looked up and into the dark eyes of a man in torn clothing. "Well, are you going to eat it or not?" he asked hoarsely.

"No," Kathleen said in a small voice.

In a flash, the man scooped up the burger and disappeared into the crowd.

Deciding she felt safer inside the station, Kathleen went back. She had just stepped into the main lobby when she spotted someone unexpected.

It was Annie Tuzmarti.

Annie wasn't alone. Desdemona, Sylvie, Rosa, Sharon, Sasha, and Lori were at the station, too. Kathleen tried to duck into the crowd, but Annie spotted her. "What's the big idea?" Annie asked, coming up to Kathleen.

"How did you guys find me?" Kathleen asked.

"Never mind that now," said Desdemona. "We want to know where you think you're going."

"I'm going on a trip," Kathleen said, sitting down on one of the benches. "For a visit, to see some friends."

"You're running away from home, you mean," said Sharon.

Kathleen didn't want to admit that they were right. They might tell her parents. "I'm not running anywhere," she said. "I'm visiting friends."

"You are too running away," Desdemona said.

"Won't your parents be upset?" Sylvie asked.

Kathleen gave up trying to lie. "I guess so," she replied. "But I'm going to write them when I get where I'm going. They've had a lot of stuff on their minds lately. I'll be one less thing for them to worry about."

"You're wrong," said Rosa. "That's not how parents feel about their children."

"How would you know?" Kathleen snapped.

"Because they love you," Rosa insisted. "You can tell just from knowing you that your parents love you. You're a nice person. You wouldn't have turned out that way if your parents didn't love you."

Rosa's words made sense. In her heart, Kathleen knew they loved her. Even though Mama was strict and Papa hadn't paid much attention to her lately, they cared about her a lot.

"You think I'm a nice person?" Kathleen asked. She'd thought they all hated her after what had happened.

"Like, duh!" Sharon scoffed. "No, we're all here because we hate your guts."

"Of course we think you're nice. That's what we came to your apartment to tell you," Annie said, sitting down beside her. "We had an emergency meeting of the DO GOODERS to talk about getting a new president."

"Fine with me," Kathleen muttered.

"No," Annie continued. "Because the more we talked, the more we saw that you did the right thing. *We* were wrong, not you. We shouldn't have picked a fight with Ronnie. That's not what the DO GOODERS was formed to do. We're the Girls' Order of Defenders, not fighters."

"That would make us the GOOFERS," Rosa pointed out. Everyone laughed.

"We *were* the goofers today," said Sylvie.

"Which is what we were going to tell you. But then *you* goofed and ran away from home," Sharon added.

"I'm running *to* home," Kathleen corrected her. "Back to Cross Corners."

"Whatever," said Sharon. "But if you ask me, that's pretty dumb. You can't just pick up and run away when stuff happens. Where would you go? Who would buy you clothes, and videos, and junk food? I don't think you really thought this through."

Kathleen had to admit that Sharon was

right. Even though she wasn't that concerned with clothes, videos, and junk food, she hadn't planned things out much. Cross Corners just seemed like this wonderful, glowing place that would be there waiting to welcome her back. But maybe she'd been wrong. Maybe she still needed her family, school, money, and a real place to live—even in Cross Corners. "How did you all know I was here?" Kathleen asked again.

"Your aunt told us," said Sasha.

Kathleen looked at her in surprise. "How did she know? I didn't tell her."

"She told us when we came to your house to talk to you. She said she'd looked out the window and saw you going down the street with your pack," Lori explained. "She knew something was wrong. She told us you were talking about going back to Cross Corners. She went out in her van to try to find you. But we hopped on the subway and got here first."

Desdemona checked her purple plastic watch. "It's seven o'clock. She's probably been stuck in rush-hour traffic all this time."

"Do you mean that all of you came on the subway to look for me?" Kathleen asked.

"Yeah. We told our parents we were all studying at Rosa's house," said Annie. "They wouldn't let us take the subway all the way over here if they knew. Keep your fingers crossed that no one's parents call Rosa's house to check."

"I'd better be home by eight or my mother *will* call," Lori said.

"Come on," said Annie. "You've got to come back with us."

"Why?" Kathleen asked.

"You're our friend," said Annie. "You— you're…like…a heroine. You stood up to Ronnie, and to us. I'm sorry for what I said in McCracken's class today. About you standing by while someone else got creamed, I mean."

"Yes," added Rosa. "You'd make a great white blood cell."

"You've got to come back," Sylvie pleaded. "You can't live without your family. Besides, they'd really miss you."

"And your friends would miss you, too," said Annie.

Friends. If they'd come all this way for her, Kathleen thought, maybe they really were her friends.

Just then, Kathleen saw Aunt Jessie running across the waiting room. "Thank heavens!" she cried, throwing her arms around Kathleen. "I've been so worried, Kath. I almost called the police, but I was hoping I could find you myself. I know you were disappointed that I wasn't going back to Cross Corners, but I never thought you'd go by yourself. I'm so sorry. I guess you must feel so terrible. I mean, I let you down, just like your friends."

At that moment, Aunt Jessie looked up and saw the DO GOODERS. "Well, maybe they haven't let you down," she said, smiling. "Come on, Kathleen. It's time for all of us to get home."

"Is Mama super-angry?" Kathleen asked.

"She knows you went out, but she doesn't know where you were going," said Aunt Jessie. "And she knows that you went out without asking. So she'll probably act mad when you get back. You know how she is. But believe me, it would break her heart to lose you. Your dad, too."

"I told you so," said Desdemona.

Kathleen picked up her backpack. Somehow Cross Corners suddenly seemed as if it might be lonely now. No one who really mattered to her lived there anymore. She saw that now. Home wasn't just a place. Home was where the people who cared about you were.

"I'd better see if I can get my money back

on this train ticket," she said.

"All right!" Annie cheered. "Way to go."

"Keep your ticket," said Aunt Jessie. "On the way here—while I was stuck in traffic—"

"I told you she was stuck in traffic," Desdemona cut in.

"Anyway, I had a great idea," Aunt Jessie continued. "You and I can take a trip back to Cross Corners for a visit some weekend. We can see everyone and everything we love about the place. Maybe we can even take a class with Mr. Funakoshi."

"Okay," Kathleen said, smiling. "Aunt Jessie, could you give my friends a ride home?"

Aunt Jessie nodded. "It'll be crowded, but I think we can make it. That is, if I haven't been towed away by now. There is no place to park a van in this city."

"What do you think Mama will say?" Kathleen asked Aunt Jessie as they all walked out of the train station.

"I don't know," her aunt replied. "I think you should tell her the truth, though. She should know where you were going."

"Do I really have to tell her?" Kathleen asked.

"She's your mother," said Aunt Jessie. "You should tell her how you've been feeling.

Don't worry. I'll stay with you if you want me to."

Kathleen nodded. She knew she needed someone on her side. Aunt Jessie understood. But facing her mother was going to be tough.

13

Kathleen was prepared for anger—even for punishment. She never expected her mother to hug her. And she certainly didn't expect her to cry.

The minute Kathleen walked in the door, Mrs. Stoppelmeyer had thrown her arms around her and burst into tears. "I was so worried, Kathleen," she sobbed. "Where have you been?"

Slowly Kathleen explained that she'd been headed back to Cross Corners.

"You went all the way to the station by yourself?" her mother gasped. "When I think what could have happened." Her mother closed her eyes and took a deep breath. "Oh, this is all my fault. I haven't been paying enough attention to you lately."

"I just really wanted to go home, Mama," said Kathleen.

"I understand how you feel," her mother said with a sigh. "I feel the same way."

"You do?" Kathleen asked in surprise.

"Yes, and I should have realized how you felt. But I've been so worried about money, and so busy trying to sell those stupid magazines…"

"You mean you want to go home?" Kathleen asked.

Her mother nodded sadly. "I've lived on a farm all my life. It's hard to get used to the city. But I thought you were making friends, Kathleen."

"I am," Kathleen replied.

"That's good," said Mrs. Stoppelmeyer, wiping her eyes.

Just then Kathleen's father burst in the door. "I can't find her any—" He cut himself short when he laid eyes on Kathleen. He walked over to her and hugged her tight.

"She was heading back to Cross Corners," Mrs. Stoppelmeyer told him. "Jess caught up with her at the train station."

"Cross Corners?" he asked. He looked at Aunt Jessie. "How did you know to look for her at the station, Jessie?"

"She's been talking about wanting to go home for a while now," Aunt Jessie answered quietly. "It seemed like the logical place to look."

Mr. Stoppelmeyer nodded. "That was a crazy thing to do, Kathleen," he said evenly. "Promise me you won't ever do anything like that again."

"I promise," said Kathleen.

"Kathleen, you have a bruise on your head," Mrs. Stoppelmeyer said, frowning. "What happened?"

Kathleen and Aunt Jessie told her parents what had happened in the cemetery. Mr. Stoppelmeyer's face went red. "Where do these girls live?" he asked.

"I don't know," Kathleen said. "On the other side of the park, I think, near the cemetery."

"Well, we're writing a letter to your teacher," said Mrs. Stoppelmeyer.

"I don't know if that's a good idea," said Kathleen.

"It is, Kathleen," Aunt Jessie insisted gently. "Trust us."

"All right," Kathleen said. She realized she *did* trust them. And she loved them too. How had she ever thought she could live without her family?

The phone rang. It was Martin checking to

see if Kathleen had come home. "Tell Adam and Sean they can stop looking, too," Aunt Jessie told Martin. "She's here and she's fine."

"Your mother and I both miss the farm," Mr. Stoppelmeyer said to Kathleen. "We miss it more than you can imagine. But our life is here now. We have to make the best of it."

"I know that," said Kathleen in a small voice.

"Go wash up for supper," said Mrs. Stoppelmeyer.

Kathleen practically skipped to the bathroom. She had suddenly remembered she was hungry. And she was glad to be home, glad to be where there were people who loved her and good food on the table.

"Kathleen," her mother called gently.

Kathleen turned. "What, Mama?"

"As much as we miss the farm, it's nothing compared to the way we would miss you if you ever left us. A farm is just a place. But you are our Kathleen. Nothing could ever replace you."

Kathleen ran to her mother and threw her arms around her. Then she felt her father's strong, rough hand on her shoulder. Parkside would never be Cross Corners, but Kathleen finally felt she was where she belonged.

The next day, Kathleen didn't find it quite as hard to get up for school. She knew her friends were waiting for her. She also knew Ronnie would leave her alone. Aunt Jessie had definitely scared her, at least for now.

She picked up the note her parents had written together and signed. It said:

> *Dear Ms. McCracken,*
> *The other day our daughter*
> *Kathleen was assaulted on the way*
> *home from school by three girls in*
> *your class named Ronnie, Jodi, and*
> *Cheryl. While we know this didn't*
> *happen on school property, we want*
> *you to be aware of the situation. We*
> *are very upset and anxious to*
> *discuss this with you and the*
> *principal. We would like to make*
> *sure this never happens again.*
> > *Sincerely,*
> > *Mr. and Mrs. Stoppelmeyer*

Kathleen was a little nervous about handing the note in, but she was going to do it anyway.

She walked down the stairs with her brothers and rapped on Aunt Jessie's door. The locks clanked open and Aunt Jessie appeared in the doorway in her robe. "Wait a minute, Kath," she said. "I have something for you."

She disappeared into her apartment for a moment and came back with a stack of light blue fliers. "Could you pass these out at school? Some of the kids might be interested."

Kathleen read the top flier.

> *The YMCA is proud to announce the formation of a beginners' karate class. All boys and girls age eight and up are welcome. We will stress physical fitness and self-defense. No experience is needed.*

"Is this your new class?" Kathleen asked.

"Yep," Aunt Jessie replied with a smile. "Hey, if your friends take this class, maybe they won't need you to fight their battles."

Kathleen's eyes brightened. "Great idea!"

"And I could use an assistant," Aunt Jessie went on. "I could only pay you a dollar an hour, but—"

"I'd do it for nothing!" Kathleen said excitedly. "All I need is for you to pay Sean back the three dollars I borrowed from him."

"Done," said Aunt Jessie.

With a spring in her step, Kathleen hurried down the stairs to catch up with her brothers. The sun was shining, and the rain had washed Willow Street clean. Today the street almost looked as if it deserved its pretty name.

Kathleen walked with her brothers as far as Grant Avenue. As they turned off to go toward school, Kathleen looked in the opposite direction. Up by Newton's Newsstand she saw her friends. "See ya," she said to her brothers as she ran to meet up with her friends.

"Hi!" she called.

"Hi," said Sylvie. "How did things go at home?"

"Great," Kathleen said. "I didn't get in trouble or anything. They were really glad to see me."

"No fair," Sharon griped. "You didn't get punished, but I'm grounded. My mother *did* call Rosa's. I walked in just as she was about to call the police."

"I'm grounded, too," said Rosa with a sigh.

"And I have dish cleanup duty for a week," added Lori. "Sharon's mother called mine."

"My mother called, too," said Annie. "But I just got off with having to go to bed early."

"Sorry, guys," Kathleen said sincerely. "I know you did it for me. I'm sorry you got in trouble."

"It's okay," Sharon said. "My groundings never last long. I drive my parents nuts until they unground me. It works every time."

"My parents don't believe in punishment," said Sasha. "They say life gives out its own rewards and punishments."

"You're lucky," said Lori. "Can you get them to talk to my parents?"

John, Carlos, and Kareem came out of Newton's with boxes of juice. "Hey, Kathleen," Kareem said.

"Listen," said John. "I'm sorry about the other day. I got a little carried away."

"He always gets carried away," Annie teased.

John jabbed his knuckle into Annie's arm. She yelped.

"That's okay," said Kathleen. But as she spoke, she saw Ronnie coming up the street. She tensed, ready for whatever might happen next. One by one, all the girls noticed Ronnie approaching.

"Ignore her," Sylvie advised.

"If she'll let us," said Desdemona grimly.

But Ronnie just crossed the street.

"I'm shocked," said Annie. "Totally shocked."

"That's weird," said Desdemona. "You don't fight her and she goes away."

"She's probably afraid because she saw me," John boasted.

"Yeah?" Carlos teased. "She's afraid she's going to have to push you over again."

"Who cares why she crossed the street?" said Kareem. "Just be glad she did."

"It's because Kathleen didn't fight her," said Desdemona. "I'm telling you, Ronnie is totally confused. She doesn't know what to expect."

Kathleen just smiled. She decided to let them think that had worked—not that Aunt Jessie had scared the daylights out of Ronnie in the cemetery. There was one thing she did feel the need to clear up, though. "You know the other day when I told you I fought wild dogs in the park?"

"Yeah," said Annie.

"Well, there were dogs, but I didn't fight them. I just threw something at them and they ran away."

"I knew that wasn't true," said Sharon.

"You did not, Sharon," said Desdemona. "You had goose bumps all over you."

"I did not," Sharon said.

"Why did you lie to us?" Sylvie asked Kathleen.

"Because I wanted you all to like me," Kathleen confessed. "And I knew you liked it that I could do karate and protect you."

Annie put her hand on Kathleen's shoulder. "That was true, at first. But then we got to know you. And we shouldn't have depended on you so much. The next time something happens, we'll all jump in and help."

"That reminds me," said Kathleen. She pulled Aunt Jessie's fliers from her backpack. "My aunt is teaching this karate class and I'm going to help her." She passed each of them a flier.

"Cool!" cried Desdemona.

"I'll sign up," said Annie.

"Me, too," said Sasha.

"And me," agreed Sylvie.

"Well, I guess if everyone else is, I will," Sharon added.

"I am definitely signing up for this," said John. "I've always wanted to learn karate."

"Well, I'll have to ask my parents," said Rosa. "But I think it would be a good idea for all of us to sign up. Then the DO GOODERS would be a real club."

Annie began leaping through the air, doing fake karate steps. John, Carlos, and Kareem joined her. "How are we doing?" she asked Kathleen.

"It's a start," Kathleen said with a smile.

They walked toward school together, cutting through Harry Park. The park looked beautiful to Kathleen once again.

In the background, a siren blared. Kathleen would never get used to that sound. But today she heard something new. Somewhere a fire was being put out. Or a sick person was being rushed to the hospital. Or someone breaking the law was being stopped.

Every minute, someone in the city was being helped. The city was full of DO GOOD-ERS. The sirens were proof of that. For the first time ever, Kathleen felt like part of the city.

She dropped her pack on the grass and began to run. Then she bounded up and did a forward flip in the air.

Don't miss the next book in the
McCracken's Class series:

McCracken's Class #5:
TOUGH LUCK, RONNIE

"You'd make a wonderful student tutor," Ms.
McCracken told Rosa. "Think of the joy in
working with one of your classmates!"

Rosa said nothing. She worked on projects
with her classmates all the time. Usually she
got stuck doing all the work. Then everyone
called her a geek.

"Ms. Santiago," the teacher went on, "I
know you enjoy a challenge."

"Well, yes," said Rosa slowly.

"And you're the only student whom I'd ask
to take on such an assignment."

"Really?" Rosa said. Why was Ms.
McCracken buttering her up like this?

"Will you at least give it a try?" Ms.
McCracken asked.

"I'll do my best," Rosa told her. Then she
hesitated. "So who am I going to be tutoring?"

Ms. McCracken smiled. "Why, the person
who most needs your help. Ronnie Smith."